MEMORIES
OF RAIN

Also by Sunetra Gupta:

The Glassblower's Breath

MEMORIES
OF RAIN

➤ • ◄

Sunetra Gupta

GROVE PRESS
New York

Grove Press
841 Broadway
New York, NY 10003-4793

Published in Canada by
General Publishing Company, Ltd.

"The Marina" from *Collected Poems 1909–1962* by T. S. Eliot. Copyright © 1936 by Harcourt Brace Jovanovich, Inc.; copyright © 1963, 1964 by T. S. Eliot. Reprinted by permission of the publisher.

Poetry of Rabindranath Tagore translated from the Bengali by the author.

Library of Congress Cataloging-in-Publication Data

Gupta, Sunetra.
    Memories of rain / Sunetra Gupta.—1st ed.
    I. Title.
    PR9499.3.G8957M46   1992
    823—dc20   91-31684

ISBN 0-8021-3341-X (pb.)

Manufactured in the United States of America
Printed on acid-free paper
Designed by Joyce Weston
First Evergreen Edition 1993

1 3 5 7 9 10 8 6 4 2

To My Mother

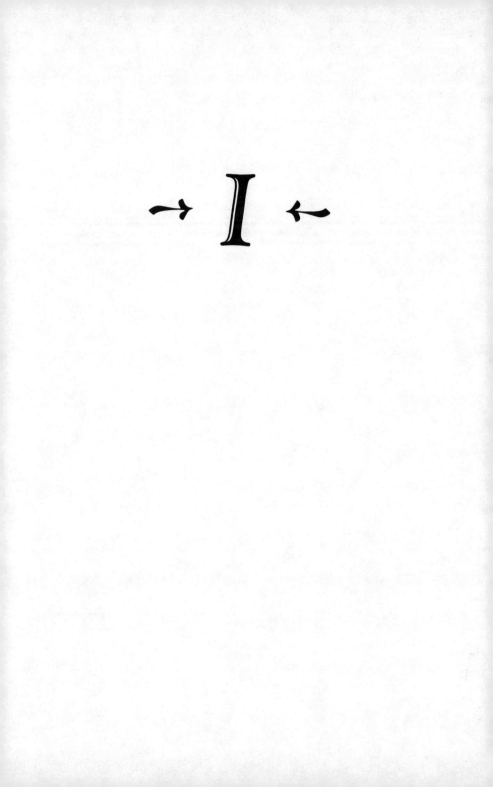

She saw, that afternoon, on Oxford Street, a woman crushing ice cream cones with her heels to feed the pigeons. She saw her fish out from a polythene bag a plastic tub that she filled with water for the pigeons, water that they would not be able to drink, for pigeons, her grandmother had told her many years ago, can only quench their thirst by opening their beaks to drops of rain. And she remembered a baby starling that, in the exhilaration of her first English spring, she had reached to hold, her hands sheathed in yellow kitchen gloves, for within her, as her husband had once observed, compassion had always been mingled with disgust.

Even he, the first time she ever set eyes upon him, had disgusted and fascinated her, the dark hairs plastered to his chalk-white legs, for this was in the flood of '78, and he had just waded through knee-deep water, he and her brother, all the way from the Academy of Fine Arts to their house in Ballygunge. He had rolled up his jeans revealing his alabaster calves which dripped the sewage of Calcutta onto the floor of their veranda, and that was what caused her to tremble in excitement and loathing as she pushed aside the curtain with a tray of tea and toast, his large, corpse-white, muck-rinded toes pushed against the bamboo table, soiling the mats she had crocheted in school. She set down the tea, her brother did not bother to introduce her, but Anthony asked, is this your sister? And she had nodded vaguely and smiled, picked up the book that she had been reading all afternoon, there on the veranda, all afternoon, watching the rain. In her room, which she shared with her grandmother, the moldy smell of a deep, long rain was settling in, compounded by the muddy strokes of the maid, who had picked this unlikely hour to wash the floors. She treaded gingerly across and flung open the shutters, letting in a spray of rain. Her grandmother, coming in with the sewing machine, pleaded with her to shut them, her old bones would freeze, she said, so she drew them in again and switched on the much-despised fluorescent light, and lay with her face towards the damp wall, lulled by the whirr of the sewing machine, and the ever loudening beat of the rain-drops, until the lights went out, as they did every night, and every morning—the inevitable power rationing—and she was summoned to take out to her brother and his white friend a kerosene light. And so she appeared to him a second time, lantern-lit, in the damp darkness, a phantom of beauty, and his eyes roamed for a time after she had disappeared inside, the ghost of light that her presence had left, there beside him, in the rain-swollen dark. He saw her again at dinner, candlelit, their first dinner, and she sat well back in the darkness, so that he could only gaze upon the flames that danced upon her delicate fingers, the drapes of her sari that fell upon the formica tabletop, and as they were being served yogurt, the lights came on again, the house sprang into action, the fans whipped up the clammy cold air, the water pump revived, Beethoven resumed on the record player. I'd rather you didn't leave the player on during load shedding, said their father, their grandmother shivered, the rain will go on for a few days now, she said, I can feel it in my bones, those poor villagers.

She noticed he had changed into some clothes of her brother's, the long punjabi shirts that he wore over jeans or loose paijama pantaloons, which together with his thick beard (gnat-infested, I'm sure, she would tease him, a veritable ecosystem, their ornitholgist uncle called it) set him apart as a man of letters, reaffirmed his association with an experimental theater group. Last year her brother had visited her in London, he had been touring in Germany, and he had sat all day in his hideous check jacket which he always kept on, in front of the television, smelling of alcohol, Anthony had had no patience with him, they were glad when he left. And yet, the first evening that he was here, the two of them had sat and argued late into the night, and she had felt again the soggy wind of that first rain-filled evening upon her limbs, as she folded clothes in the laundry room, their voices drifting towards her, the quivering ring of heat around the edges of the iron. Later as she lay upstairs staring through the bedroom curtains at the haze of the streetlights, their voices rose in thin wisps to edge the darkness, as they had done that moldy evening, when all of Calcutta was one large sea of mud and dung, and floating waterlogged Ambassador cars, and children disappeared on their way home from school into open manholes, their covers wrenched off and sold long ago, to drown in the city's choked sewers, on a night like this, he had come to dinner, and been forced to stay, she had been ordered to spread clean sheets on her brother's bed in the living room, which during the day they called the divan, and make one up on the floor for her brother, and so she heard them talk, wide-eyed in the dark of her own bedroom, heard their laughter amid the gentle snores of her grandmother, the vacillating rain. She heard her brother's footsteps, the corridor light came on, she heard him rummaging at his desk, which lay in an alcove in the corridor where, as children, they had kept their toys, the little red tricycle that they rode together on the roof terrace, the silver-haired dolls her aunt sent from Canada. She emerged cautiously from her bedroom to meet his excited eyes.

"You're not asleep yet!" he exclaimed.

"You woke me up," she retorted, but he brushed by her

without a rejoinder, she struggled with the heavy latch on the bathroom door until it slid down suddenly, as it always did, and once within, she stood in the mossy darkness, and heard through the thin walls her brother translating to his English friend a play that he had just finished writing last week, his first (there, he had said to her, a week ago, after an afternoon of furious scribbling, what do you think, do you think your brother will make it as a playwright, tell me, Moni, if this isn't better than most of the crap that they call theater, and she had put down her Agatha Christie novel to pick up with her calm fingers the foolscap booklet that he had flung on the bed, at her feet), the play was set in rural West Bengal, where, her brother had wanted to show, the peasantry were still as oppressed as they had been the past thousand years under feudalism, you must take me out there, she heard Anthony say, you must acquaint me with rural Bengal, that was what she had heard him say, her cheeks pressed against the damp bathroom walls, on a night of mad thunder and rains that swept away half the peasantry of their land, left them without the mud walls within which they had sheltered their grains, their diseased children, their voracious appetites, and their stubborn ignorance. For she had come to this island, this demi-paradise, from a bizarre and wonderful land, so Anthony's friends called it, was it true, they asked, that they still burn their wives, bury alive their female children? And she would nod numbly, although she had known only of those children that had escaped death, whether deliberate or from disease, those that had been sent out to serve tea in tall grimy glasses in roadside stalls, or to pluck the gray hairs of obese turmeric-stained metropolitan housewives, fill the gentleman's hookah, blow, blow until the green flame gushes, while the mother, helpless domestic, watches silently and trembles. And even these were often graven images, culled from film and fiction. From such a land Anthony had rescued her, a land where the rain poured from the skies not to purify the earth, but to spite it, to churn the parched fields into festering wounds, rinse the choked city sewers onto the streets, sprinkle the pillows with the nausea of mold, and yet the poet had pleaded with the deep green shadows of the rain clouds not to abandon him, the very same poet who wrote,

> You, who stand before my door in this darkness
> Who is it that you seek?
> It has been many years since that spring day, when there came
>   a young wanderer
> And immersed my parched soul in an endless sea of joy;
> Today, I sit in the rain-filled darkness, in my crumbling shack
> A wet wind snuffs my candle, I sit alone, awake;
> Oh, unknown visitor, your song fills me with sweet awe
> I feel I will follow you to the depths of uncharted dark.

But it was not this song, not yet, that ran through her rain-ravaged mind as the grandfather clock in the living room struck two, interrupting the awkward flow of her brother's translation, the grammatical mistakes she shivered at, why was his English so terrible, and she stood in the bathroom, splashed icy cold water out of the drum onto her feet, she caught a ghost of herself in the cracked mirror, and a sudden embarrassment overcame her, she switched on the lights and took in the cracked plaster, the dilapidated water closet, long since choked with lime, suspended over the Turkish toilet, the cracked mirror, the shelf cluttered with bottles of coconut oil, toothpaste tubes, rusty razor blades, and she compared it to the bathrooms at Amrita's, where she knew Anthony was staying, marbled to the ceiling, with Western commodes and bathtubs, he cannot be used to any of this, she thought, and now as she luxuriated in the lavender-scented heat of her bath, she would wonder how she had ever been used to it either. Yet, for many years, that bathroom had been her only refuge, here she had soaped the corners of her growing body, watched her breasts bud, shampooed the grime of the city out of her long black hair, memorized poems with her face to the knife-edged drops of water from the shower, and that night, before she drew back the latch and stepped into the corridor, she whispered to herself from Keats' "Ode on Melancholy," which they had dissected that afternoon in her Special Paper class, and saw in her mind's eye Anthony, crushing grapes with his strenuous tongue against his palate fine: his soul shall taste the sadness of her might, and be among her cloudy trophies hung.

She was jerked awake in the morning by her mother, it was still raining, the floodwater lapped at the outside walls, but somehow, even in all this, her father had managed to procure a whole chicken on his daily morning excursion to the market. On her way to the bathroom, she glimpsed the sleeping form of her brother, one dark arm grazing the floor, and for once, she shared the indignation of her uncles that it was still her father who went to the market every morning while he slept off his late nights, but let the boy sleep, their father would protest, I go for my morning walk anyway, it doesn't hurt me to stop by the bazaar, besides he is the artistic type, he does not comprehend life's practicalities. So who does the shopping now, who braves the early-morning sun to haggle over fish, fish smeared with goat blood to simulate freshness, you shake the flies from your face and palpate the aubergines, the king prawns are a hundred rupees a kilo today, but nothing is too good for my daughter's wedding, even if she is marrying an Englishman, they will still have it done the traditional way, that was all her father had asked of her. You alone are to blame for the ruin of your children, her uncles would tell him later, you indulged them, and now as you sit paralyzed in your grandfather's rocking chair, your son lies sodden with drink at the Press Club and your daughter is lost to you, over the seas.

And yet that rain-laden morning, her mother had allowed her to wander through the living room in her nightdress, which she never would have tolerated if any other friend of her brother's had been asleep on the moist floor, but he, this white man, was too remote to be a threat, there was no need for modesty, and so she looked upon him, as he slept, the dark eyebrows, deep-set eyes, closed now, the sunburned chin, he did not look quite so European as those Germans that had been here last year, he could almost pass for a North Indian, but for that peculiar papery texture of his scorched skin. She brought in tea, and her brother sat up suddenly rubbing his eyes, but Anthony rolled over, turned his face to the wall, and continued to sleep the sleep of the dead, as he would later in the face of her despair, gray mornings through pale curtains, the finality of his striped pajama back.

"So what should I do with his tea?" she asked her brother.

"Leave it, if he doesn't get up I'll drink it."

The roar of thunder drowns the faint tinkle of rickshaw bells. Thick wet footsteps on the veranda, an umbrella shaken and opened out to dry, the smell of betel juice drifts through the damp air, her music tutor has arrived, on a morning like this, he picks his muddy way past the white man, glances at him with disgust, she leads him into the bedroom, pulls out the grass mat, all smells are magnified in this grand penetrating wetness. She drags out the harmonium from under the bed, the keys are moist with condensation, the notes slice through the damp air, her brother slams the bathroom door. She pulls out the heavy volume of Tagore songs, opens it to the right page, it is a song of rain that she has been learning these past few weeks, she has almost mastered it, but for a few delicate folds in the final phrases. Her tutor runs a gnarled finger across the lines, who but the poet

· 9 ·

could have captured the sorrow of the rain so well? he asks, as if she might have dared to suggest otherwise.

And so he woke, a strange chill in his limbs, to the sound of her windy voice, unfamiliar halftones, words he would never understand,

> in the dense obsession of this deep dark rain
> you tread secret, silent, like the night, past all eyes.

Her voice rises, she is immersed in the words he cannot understand, although they come to him like the wet morning wind:

> the heavy eyelids of dawn are lowered to the futile wail of the
>   winds
> clotted clouds shroud the impenitent sky
> birdless fields
> barred doors upon your desolate path.

He sits up, a weak cup of tea is pushed towards him, her voice rises again,

> oh beloved wanderer, I have flung open my doors to the storm
> do not pass me by like the shadow of a dream.

Many years later, huddled in a deserted tin mine on the Cornish coast, she translated the same song for him, staring into the sheets of rain that ran by like frozen phantoms across the crumbling entrance, and he sat back against the moldy walls, paying only half heed to her eager, nervous translations, mesmerized instead by the duet of the storm and the sea, until, like the sudden spray, it hit her that he was not listening, he was not listening at all, but they had been rescued, then, by the sudden urge to see their child, the girl left behind at his mother's, was she staring glumly into the rain, her little elbows on the white sill, or was she wrapped up in her grandmother's lap, rocking back and forth to a story, her cold toes digging into the old woman's wrinkled palms. Wedged between two Swedish cars on the Cornish moorland motorway, she had watched the rhythm of her breath as it condensed on the car window, while he had mused of his afternoon with Anna, a curious half-smile flitting across his face from time to time, for he had long come to terms with his infidelity, he implored her silently, ever, to accept it, to reconcile the poetry of his passion for Anna with his deep affection for her and for her child, as he had done, after many evenings of gentle agony, desperately curling the child's hair in his agitated fingers, the unbearable stillness of a rare summer evening, her regular breathing, a child asleep on a summer evening, sun-warmed sheets billowing in the garden. The doorbell rings, she staggers in with the shopping, her face flushed, he holds her in his sad embrace, I will make dinner, you sit down and rest, and as they eat their scrambled eggs, he looks across at her in the dying light, that beloved darkness in the hollows of her eyes, perhaps she was what really held them together, Anna and himself, without her, there would be no substance to their relationship, he remembers a night, drenched with lavender, in the hills of Provence, where, among the olive groves, he had first kissed Anna's warm lips, he remembers his sad exhilaration grappling with an emotion long forgotten, an emotion that is there but in faint wisps, on the winding path back to the rented cottage he is divided between an excruciating guilt and an insane desire to preserve the passion that having climaxed in that one painful kiss seems now to be melting away. In the distance, he can hear Moni singing, she sits by the window, her song drifting towards them with the spiced winds, her foreign lament, was it sad, was it joyful, it was her song that had hypnotized them then, infused them with a gentle sustained lust, that was, perhaps, their doom,

in this moonlit night, they have all gone wandering in the forest
in this mad springtime wind, in this moonlit night

for the lush warmth of the South of France had taken her back
to moonlit college picnics by broad tropical rivers, the spell of
her song webbed across the wide fields

I will not go into the inebriated spring winds
I will sit alone, content, in this corner
I will not go forth into the drunken winds

—the inscrutable elation of the poet, who shall not sip of the
wild honey of spring, for he awaits a sterner intoxication, and he
must remain watchful, lest those that wander in the forest
should choke upon the spring breezes and the moonlight, the
poet must remain awake,

in this moonlit night, they have gone wandering in the forest
drunk with the young wind of springtime.

She turns around to face them, dense shadows in the doorway,
a shadow shifts and sighs, Anna is beside her, the moonlight
fringes her wet lashes, and Anthony moves quietly to her other
side, they have surrounded her, for one perfect moment she is
an integral part of their passion, they are circled by love. And it
had become clear to her, as they picked their way through the
gorges of the Ardèche, where the butterflies swirled like pieces
of burnt paper, that this was no temporary lust, no flitting desire
worked by the lavender breezes and the moonlight, no mild
weekend enchantment that he would work off by listening to
Mozart all day, these she had grown to tolerate, but here, among
the charred butterflies, like a thin stream of blood in her mouth,
came the first taste of her long tryst with fear. How would it

happen, she wondered, would he seat her down gently, and explain, stroking with a kind hand, her long black hair, his other hand strumming on an airplane ticket, and how could she ever go home, home to the wild grief of her parents, the snickers of the neighbors, her brother's pity, his smugness—but no, how could he be smug, he who turned away his cloudy eyes at the airport, think of what you will miss, Moni, think of what you are giving up, how can you desert us like this, Moni? For he had been so terribly proud of her, her voice, her talents, his friends' roving eyes as she served them tea, her refinement, he had molded her, told her what to read, how to appreciate it, taken her with him to plays and films, the right films, forbidden her to accompany her girlfriends to the trashy commercial films they all went giggling to see, not that he needed to, she and her group of close friends preferred English films anyway, he would drag her off to the film societies to see French and German films, Russian films, and now, she would surprise a group of Anthony's friends with a shy, yes, I have seen that, amid conversations where her only other contribution was her smile. A moment of silence, all eyes upon her, someone would ask kindly, how did you like it, trying to draw her into the conversation. Anthony would smile encouragingly, and she would voice some simple opinion and if they were in the mood they would try and tease some more out of her, but soon enough a rapid and incomprehensible debate would erupt, and she would get up to make the coffee. She did not mind it this way, indeed this was what she had been used to at home, among her brother's friends, opinionated, enthusiastic, they were terrifying, the stern, beautiful Amrita, the rotund Gayatri who always played the mother with her glorious, deep voice, the men, all in beards, blur in her mind now, she would sit among them, as she did here, now, among Anthony's friends, silent, smiling, absorbing their life, their determination, their warmth. Would she have become like them, like Amrita, confident and eloquent, had she stayed there? Had she been arrested in her development, remained the passive, attentive child, by crossing the seas to an unfamiliar country, where, despite her half-finished honors degree in English, she could not find the right words, the right expressions, to voice her opinions, to participate but in the most banal of conversations, or was she merely passive by nature, content to sit and listen? Might she have burgeoned, shed the role of the adolescent sister, nurtured by their admiration, their respect? In the summer months before Anthony came to Calcutta, they had invited her to sing a few Tagore songs, offstage, for one of their plays, it was her entrance to their world, she loved the smoky school hall where they rehearsed in North Calcutta, she would look out of the tall windows onto the narrow gutter-lined streets where the little boys played cricket, square-cutting balls into the gutter, to be fished out gingerly and washed under the burst hydrants, the mossy courtyards where their mothers waited with glasses of milk that they gulped and ran out again like a shot to join the game, and then some gentle hand would fall upon her shoulder, could you sing "Je ratey mor duarguli" for us now? Pull out the off-key harmonium, Ranjan fiddles with the tabla, knocking about with a hammer, all right then, Polash has the tape recorder ready, you may begin, Moni,

> On the night that my doors broke with the storm
> How was I to know that you would appear at my door?
> A blackness surrounded me, my light died
> I reached towards the sky, who knows why?

Her voice echoes through the old school hall, which creaks every morning under hundreds of fidgety feet, identically shod, the sound of fluttering hymn books, corners that have been creased a century ago by careless sunburned fingers. Later, when they are all eating lunch, spicy meat in earthenware containers, with paper-thin rumali roti, "handkerchief bread," she tries out the old piano, we should have used this rather than that wretched harmonium, she remarks. Gayatri, swinging her legs from the stage, asks her to eat something, but she shakes her head, she suspects that the meat is beef, she knows that they all eat beef, and that the food has been bought from the Muslim restaurant down the road. Her brother teases her about her conservative Brahmanic habits, and embarrassed, she retires to a corner of the vast hall, where behind heavy, dust-smothered curtains there are worn gym horses, benches and bars, instruments of torture in the hands of some terrifying gym mistress, her heart floods with sympathy, and yet she feels detached, she is part of another world.

And now on Oxford Street watching a woman crush ice cream cones to feed the pigeons, she is seized by an overwhelming desire to return to that world, although she knows it is there for her no longer, that the experimental theater group has long been dissolved, that her brother squanders his meager journalist's income on alcohol, her mother arranges with her tired hands the disused limbs of her father over the divan in the living room, the divan which used to serve as her brother's bed, the same divan that had been offered to Anthony on that first night of incessant rain. But somehow he had ended up on the floor, perhaps the divan was not long enough to contain his vast frame, and that was where he had woken up to the rain-swollen syllables of her song, buried his face in the clammy pillow to drown his sudden burning desire to smell the rain vapor on her young skin, to run his hands through her moist cloud-black hair, there was a sound of wet feet on the floor beside him, he raised his face from the pillow to find her closing the front door, quietly, so as not to disturb him, and then to check that she had not woken him up, she turned, and so he looked upon her in the leaden morning light, tried to hide his naked desire with a smile, that she did not return, but ran past him, confused, and bumped into her brother, coming out of the bathroom.

"What's your hurry," he asked her. "I can't believe that bohonkus of a music teacher made it in this weather."

"You had better telephone Amrita," he told Anthony in English, toweling his hair as he came into the living room. "I don't think you can go back in this."

And so he had stayed, shared their midday meal of chicken and rice after showering in death-cold water, and during the thunder-filled afternoon, they had played cards on the living-room floor, two young cousins had turned up, soaked to their waists, grinning proudly, they had walked all the way from Dhakuria, and they had produced from their sodden shoulder bags several packs of cards. They played rummy, until hypnotized by the rain, they drifted off, one by one, into a leaden monsoon slumber, only he and Moni were too conscious of each other to submit to the torpor of the ponderous rain. She brought pillows for them all, and for one painful moment, he was afraid she would leave, but she sat down to finish the game. For a while, a silence between them deepened with the slap of well-worn cards on the cold damp floor, the delicate snores of the two boys, the heavy wheeze of her brother whose oily hair grazed Anthony's toes. She was across from him, leaning against an armchair, her coal-black hair spread out over the chintz seat, lifted high on either arm, a valley of hair. She had wrapped her arms in her sari, faded print flowers pushed against her chin, and from there his eyes traveled up to her overflowing lips, her remarkable eyes under dark brows,

I heard you singing this morning, he said, you have a lovely voice.

He finds out from her that she is in her second year at college, he is strangely pleased that she is studying English, he leans back against the dank pillow and asks her what she likes to read.

Oh, everything, really—poetry, novels. She likes Thomas Hardy, and Keats. They are reading Keats, now. "Ode on Melancholy."

Boldly, he begins to recite, No, no! go not to Lethe, neither twist wolf's bane, tight-rooted . . . heavy words sink between them in the bloated afternoon. She listens with closed eyes, the rain ceases and the room is suddenly flooded with a lime-colored syrupy light that deepens the shadow of her eyes. He cannot remember the rest of the poem, he asks her, could you translate to me the song you were singing this morning, it sounded so beautiful.

Oh no, she says, my English isn't good enough.

Your English is beautiful.

But she is too embarrassed. She will translate it for him, years later, in a moldy tin mine on the Cornish coast, while he is lost in the thick swirl of lovemaking recollected, feeding deeply on the fresh memories of a recent afternoon of salt-encrusted passion. And the memories that her songs bring to him now are no longer laced with bitterness, not since he found that he could bring to their bed, in peace, the warmth of another woman. Yet, her silence becomes more and more inscrutable, there is dignity in her silence, in her excruciating grief of her untranslated songs, but does anger froth behind those long stretches of silence? He will hold her for hours in the morning, kiss her sleepless eyes, he wants to ask her if she would like to go home for a visit, her parents have not seen the child yet, but he cannot for fear she will think he is sending her away, she is like a small, soft bird in his arms, he does not dare to attempt to make love to her, he prays that through her songs she will come to appreciate the beauty of their situation, the only thing that can save them now, the intense beauty of their interwoven emotions, the poetry of the half triangle they form, he, Anna, and she, evenings that the three of them spend together, Anna dries while he washes up, and she dishes the remains of their quiet dinner into freezer containers, evenings she must spend alone while he and Anna make violent love in her studio flat, he envisages her sitting in the half-light of dusk, singing, or rocking the child to sleep, images of peace. She had been afraid once, he knew, afraid he would leave her, and he had been afraid too, that he would not be able to sustain his affection for her, but it had not happened, what had seemed inevitable in the valleys of the Ardèche, among the blackened butterflies, for him at least, it had not happened.

Had it helped that on the deck of the ferry, as they approached their dreaded return to this land, she had told him she thought she was with his child. Had it become clear to him then, in a flash of sea spray, that he would love her forever, even though their passion was spent. But he had no inkling of her great relief when the doctor confirmed her pregnancy, she prayed that it would be a son, somehow a son would be a true synthesis of herself with him, an embodiment of their union, a daughter was an extension of herself, a daughter would not be his, a daughter would be hers alone. Today, as she watches the woman grinding ice cream cones underfoot, the child tugs at her arm, she wants her to look at a poodle that has found its way to the front of the bus, her lips, lollipop-rimmed, jet curls fall on her little shoulders, she is hers alone, the bus jerks, she bumps her head against the bar, but she does not cry, six years old in three more days. Anna is taking her out tomorrow to buy her a new party dress, their first outing alone, which is why, today, along with the armloads of crepe paper and crackers and balloons, they have bought a little bottle of perfume, very expensive perfume that she has seen on Anna's dressing table in the little alcove in her studio flat where she sleeps, where she makes love to her husband on apocalyptic winter evenings, she had no idea it would be so expensive, the perfume, and when they get home, she and the child will wrap it up in some of the pink crepe paper, and they will rehearse how, tomorrow, in Anna's car, after they have bought the dress, she will say, I have a present for you too, ever so sweetly, let it never be said she was not bringing up her child properly.

She can smell in the chill of the white walls of the hallway, as they fling open the door, that this will be another evening alone. She sheds her overcoat, and sits down suddenly on the bottom stair, her eyes travel up the stairway, punctuated by the large soft toys that Anthony loves to give their daughter, life-size koalas, placid teddy bears, a benign brontosaur, when she was younger she had been more scared than pleased, and to prevent nightmares they had been moved out from her room, to litter the stairs, and Anthony had found the effect so pleasing, there they had remained. Sitting there, her aching head against a soft orange kangaroo, like the first sharp smell of magnolia blossoms, a new thought penetrates her tired mind. It strikes her suddenly, in the same way it had done many years ago, in a small Chinese restaurant on Free School Street where she agreed to marry Anthony, that there was an immense pleasure to be found in escaping her present circumstances, in leaving the country forever. Ten years ago, he had pushed aside a plate of Manchurian chicken to gather into his broad hands her shy fingers, implored her to marry him, to come back with him to his home across the seas, where, for the rest of their lives, if nothing else, they could lie in each other's arms, and she would sing to him. And suddenly, it had become clear to her that this was the disaster she must embrace, like the poet, who perceived through disaster the vastness of the universe, in a train rushing through the tropical darkness, returning from the funeral of his beloved son, the universe had revealed to him its vast and indifferent beauty,

> my light has been quenched upon this dark and lonely path
> for a storm is rising

a storm is rising to befriend me
darkling disaster smiles at the edges of the sky
catastrophe wreaks delighted havoc with my garments, with my
   hair
my lamp has blown out on this lonely road
who knows where I must wander now, in this dense dark
but perhaps the thunder speaks of a new path
one that will take me to a different dawn.

A heady perfume of disaster envelops her as she sits in a dream on the number forty-seven bus, a doe-eyed child pushes against her, she draws her into her lap, the Calcutta rush hour, the weight of humankind against her knees, a hand reaches through the window, laden with books, she takes them, they are mathematics books, worn, used by many generations, and a few minutes later, the hand is back again, she closes the fingers gently over the books, she will never know him, he who, hanging from a forty-seven bus on a winter afternoon, entreated some nameless soul to hold his books for him, she will never know him, and all this she is leaving behind.

Her brother is waiting on the balcony, as if he knows, as if he expects her to tell him today, this very afternoon, that she is leaving them forever. She draws the latch on the iron grille door, sets down her bag on the bamboo table, she sits down and draws her shawl tighter as a smoky blast of damp winter wind rattles the wooden shutters. He does not look up from his book, she leans across and tips it up to see the front cover, Brecht's *Galileo*.

"Where have you been?" he asks without looking up.

The destitute call of tropical birds fills the sky, the sparrows that will crawl into the whitewashed ventilators, the crows and the kites circling the rubbish pits for a last morsel, the mynahs that gather their mates for the journey home to the dusty treetops.

"He wants to marry me," she says apologetically.

They made very little fuss, her family. The afternoon melts into evening, they sit in the living room, her mother quietly crying but making no word of protest, her father trying to concentrate on the arrangements, his one request, a proper Bengali wedding, Anthony will agree, will he not? And her grandmother is surprisingly supportive, will you take me to visit you, she asks, your grandfather always promised, but he never took me with him. It is an evening of quiet, gentle grief, nobody challenges her decision, that will come later with her irate uncles, their disgusted wives, hours of frantic weeping, a river of tears running along the formica-topped dining table. But this first evening, they sit wrapped in grief, the immediate honeyed agony of an impending partition. The doorbell sounds, she gets up to open it, it is Anthony, he sees from her face that she would rather he had not come just yet, should I leave? he asks.

No, come in. A guest can never be turned away, only salesmen are turned away, turned into the heat of parched afternoon, laden with their packets of detergent, the bottles of shampoo, the sanitary towels that they take from door to door, only salesmen are turned away.

But at the sound of his voice they have evacuated the living room. He reaches for her hand, she snatches it back, not here, not in this house. They sit for a while in the half-light, the winter evening deepens, she gets up and pushes past the dining table, through the double doors into her bedroom, where the four of them sit, huddled, silent, she pleads with them to come out into the living room, I'll be there in a minute, her brother tells her, and she rushes out again, sweet disaster, this is the shape of her delicious torment, four huddled figures in a darkened bedroom, a winter evening, the mosquitoes begin to drift in through the shutters. Her brother comes in, Anthony stands up, and suddenly the two of them laugh, a warmth of pure happiness steals over her, her brother shakes his head, so you're taking my sister from us? But we will be back every year, they both protest, and in these ten numb years, she has only been back once, alone. Later that night, her brother came up with her onto the roof terrace, where a crisp clear layer of night lay above the smoky lights of the city, and looking out onto the sea of night smoke, their impenitent city, he reminded her, this is what you are giving up, this is what you will be leaving, forever, and she raised her eyes to the hard, cold stars above, and with a voice, dark as the inside of a bird's nest, she replied, I know.

And today, ten years later, that same cold clarity floods her mind, the numbness of ten years melts suddenly away, a quantum leap in her consciousness,

> on this last night of spring, I have come empty-handed, garland-
> less
> a silent flute cries, the smile dies on your lips
> in your eyes a wet indignation
> when did this spring pass by, where is my song?

as she helps the child make paper chains, she weighs the situation carefully, a sense of drama that she has suppressed for so long enfolds her, they will leave on Monday, the morning of the birthday party, she will watch his unsuspecting face leave for the day, for the last time, oh the thrill of "the last time"—the last exam of the year, the last class, the last night of the summer holidays, the last day of the year, the last night of her brother's play, the last night of her maidenhood—her college friends encircle her, wistful, proud, nervous, so what is it like to sleep with a white man, Sharmila asked her, when she visited them two years later, and she had wrinkled her brow, averted her eyes, she had never been able to participate when they all sat together and giggled about sex in college, she could not talk about it now.

Sharmila came from a very westernized family, they spoke a queer mixture of English and Bengali at home, and the one time Anthony had intercepted her on her way back from college, in those very first days of their love, she had been walking to the bus stand with Sharmila, and it was she that conversed with him in her convent-school English as they sat in Flury's and ate chocolate eclairs. She had remained silent for the most part, enjoying the slight pressure of his knee against hers, his adoring eyes as they gazed upon her, and then flitted back to Sharmila, as he answered her incessant questions, with amusement, she had enjoyed the abstract smile that was ever upon his lips, hovering against his deep-set eyes, that was the beginning of a silent complicity, that she was, now, finally, about to violate.

As the child watches television, she telephones a travel agent, never before, since she came to this land, has she ventured to take her destiny into her own hands, not a single decision, in these ten years, she has never made any arrangements other than for dinner parties, other than getting a babysitter, other than buying birthday presents, these ten years. She pays by Anthony's credit card, her own credit limit is not high enough, she can pick up the tickets on the morning of the flight, Monday, her last morning, her last walk through the piles of dead leaves in Waterlow Park, her last ride on the C2, her last drink of water in the kitchen, she is letting her imagination, held for so long at bay, run away. Perhaps she will not be able to go through with it at all. For it is not, she reasons in her new mood of analysis, discontent, as such, that has driven her to this, there is peace in the evenings that she sits alone, by the volcanic rock fire, watching the unnatural leaps of the gas flames, the child asleep upstairs. There is a quiet understanding among the three of them on evenings that they sit together and talk into the night, even though she knows that when she creeps up the stairs to check on the child, he will take into his eager fingers Anna's smooth soft hand and between the chairs, under the blanket he has thrown over himself, their fingers will play mad havoc with each other, as theirs had, hers with Anthony's, many years ago, in the congealed, air-conditioned dark of a tropical theater, while her brother groped about on the stage as Tiresias, Amrita flamed as Jocasta, eclipsing them all, now, there was a woman, there was everything she aspired to be, and planning her departure, she feels a strange kinship with her, feels that she has finally become worthy of her respect. Perhaps, when they are in Calcutta, she will visit her in her ancient, marbled home, and tell her of her need to become whole again, and Amrita will nod her stately head, grave and beautiful, and impart to her the grace and dignity of being that she seeks. She must go where he will never find her, never set eyes again upon her, upon their child. Perhaps she would take up a post at some small village school, like her aunt, who had escaped the tortures of a cruel marriage in her tiny, whitewashed headmistress' office, shaded by squat mango trees. Tortured by her husband's family for the small dowry she had brought, she had walked out, in her bare feet, onto the baking Calcutta pavements, the melting asphalt, one rancid afternoon, she had appeared at her parents' home, like a stubborn ghost, and for five painful years she lived there, almost as a servant, struggling through college, until one bright morning, she had quietly laid a carbon copy of her appointment letter on her father's desk, packed her few belongings, and left. In remote, rural Bengal, a two-hour cycle rickshaw ride from an obscure train station, she had climbed from the ranks of a junior teacher to headmistress at the village school, Moni remembers the peculiar dryness of her skin, her gray hair pulled back into a diminutive bun, her starch-stiff clothes, her horn-rimmed glasses, a sense of desiccation that she had always associated with women without men, a concept that had terrified her then.

A winter breeze rustles the water hyacinths that choke the village ponds, Moni is reading a geography textbook by a bare window that furnishes her with the last light of the winter day, a cold light, not the soft dying rays of a spring evening that they call the light by which a maiden must be seen for the first time,

> in the dying light of that March day
> I saw in your eyes, my doom

an oft-profaned line from the Tagore novel *Char Adhyay*—"Four Quartets"—that she and Sharmila would whisper to each other against some somber sunset, alone on their terrace, with no one particular in mind, hypnotized by the dark cadence of the words. She wrote long letters to Sharmila from the village, half in English, half in Bengali, unwashed in her nightgown, bent double on her rock-hard bed in her aunt's cottage, the harsh morning sun would pierce the room, and sounds of violent pond-side laundry would lend rhythm to the torrent of emotions that she laid bare on the faded blue of inland letter forms which she sealed with a clotted glue that she always felt an irrepressible urge to taste. As she scribbled furiously, Kanan would come in with tea and a hard-boiled egg, she kept house for her aunt, Kanan, the village widow whom her aunt had rescued from a life of misery, whom she taught in the evenings, to read and write. Her brother would amble in, toweling his hair after his morning swim in the muddy ponds.

"What do you find to write about, to that tash friend of yours?" he teased her, tash friend, Anglicized, superficial, that was what he thought of Sharmila, Sharmila who spoke English with her sisters, and went dancing at the Calcutta clubs, but she had read more Bengali literature than herself, and she wrote such beautiful English and such clear Bengali, her brother would never understand.

"There is a blind beggar who sits under a gnarled tree by the river and sings the most beautiful fisherman's songs, I am tempted to ask him to teach me some. I wish I had borrowed your cassette recorder, I could have taped them for you," she writes, the royal-blue ink looks drab against the flaking swamp blue of the letter sheet, but the village store does not carry black ink, she had sulked the previous evening because she hated to write in her journal in anything but black ink, you are really silly, sometimes, her brother had told her. She had not kept a journal in years, now, not since she had found it embarrassing, difficult, and certainly too dangerous to record her meetings with Anthony, the guilt of her physical attraction, even the poetic doom of their love, all she had ever written, a hesitant entry in the red-vinyl-bound diary, now locked away in some dusty trunk under the bed upon which she had lain it, to write, on the second night of the flood, a quieter night, with a steady fine rain, an infatuating monotony,

"Dada"—her brother—"brought home a very interesting Englishman last night. He is here to study Bengali theater, it seems, how he got such an idea I do not know, and somehow I could not find the right words in English to ask him, politely, why. He is staying with Amrita, naturally. She sent a car for him at around five, I have a feeling the driver will have to push the car in this flood rather than drive it to Short Street. We talked, this afternoon, as everybody else snored away, we talked of poetry as it thundered outside. It has been raining all day, it is driving me insane . . ."

As she is screwing the cap back on her fountain pen, the lights go out, is it just the regular power cut or has the rain penetrated deep into the ground cables? Kerosene lanterns are lit, her cousins insist on playing dumb charades in the limited light, ghostly hands gesture in the turgid darkness, but she is banished from the game for her inattention, she retires to her room with a small light. She sets it upon her small desk, and delves among her textbooks for her *Selections from English Poetry*, with a strange guilt, she turns the pages to Keats' "Ode on Melancholy," she closes her eyes to recall his voice, go not to Lethe, she is glad of the darkness that envelops her, glad to lay her face against the cool rough pages without arousing attention, glad to be able to sit back in the damp shadows as they eat boiled potatoes and boiled lentils, boiled eggs with rice, and the few odd pieces left of the chicken from lunch, a gullet, a gizzard, some other inscrutable part of its anatomy, the sound of rain rises and falls, the radio crackles and fizzes in the darkness.

She cannot sleep that night, a deep nausea has taken root within her, from the damp sheets a queer alkaline odor is rising, the rain-swollen doors, that no longer close, reek of rotting termite eggs, a sea of filth laps at the walls outside. She tries to drown herself in the memory of the perfume of the first raindrops upon a dry earth, the pure smell of hot sand, of parched cotton, of saris, stiff with warmth as she picks them off the clothesline on the terrace, but the dull metronome of the raindrops has numbed her mind. She moves off the bed, and crouching on the chill cement floor, she drags from under the bed a trunk in which her mother stows their winter clothes. She burrows among the handknit pullovers, the Taiwanese acrylics, smuggled across the Nepal border, the heavy Kashmiri shawls, she digs among the folded garments for the scattered balls of naphthalene, these she gathers and lifts to her nostrils. She puts a few under her pillow, and hopes that she will sleep.

Three days later, the floodwater still stains the pavements, but a ferocious sun towers with newfound might, and sitting in her room, hemming a sari, she suddenly hears Anthony's voice, he has come to return the umbrella, an age-old ploy, she smiles and bites off the thread. She will not leave her room, she decides, wickedly amused. But before long, her brother pokes his head in.

"Make us some tea, Moni, there's a good girl," he demands.

"Make it yourself," she says, suppressing a wild excitement.

"Come on, Moni, you know I'll mess it up. Look, there's no one home, and the maid has gone to the ration shop, please, Moni."

She gives in, ties a knot in the thread. In the kitchen, she lights the gas ring, and watches the kettle rock on the hob with a strange delight. On a newspaper-lined shelf, next to the stainless-steel plates and glasses, sit the misshapen ceramic mugs that they use regularly, she cannot serve him tea in them, she decides, and picks her way across the vegetable peels that the maid has not cleared up, to the glass cabinet against the far wall. In there, among the cobwebs, nestles the delicate tea set that her aunt brought back from Canada for her mother, many years ago. A cockroach climbs out of the cup that she reaches for and she recoils in horror, but it must be done, she wrinkles her nose and picks out three cobwebbed cups, three dusty saucers. She washes them as the tea soaks, and unable to locate a clean cloth, dries the outsides with the loose end of her sari.

"Won't you join us?" Anthony asked her, hopefully, as she picked up her cup and made as to return to her room, having set down the tray with a thud and a rattle on the cluttered coffee table. But she shook her head, made some excuse, and left, she was satisfied, he had come in the hope of seeing her, this she had confirmed, now in the quiet of her room she would relish his disappointment.

An hour later, he has not gone, and she is beginning to get restless. Suddenly, her brother pokes his head in again.

"We are going to see *Citizen Kane* at the USIS. Want to come?"

And so, in the refrigerated halls of the American Center, he manages to sit beside her and cast sidelong glances at her profile, enchanting in the luminosity of the reflecting screen. After the film, they take a taxi to Amrita's house, where they have tea and cutlets in her study. Suddenly, she is curious, how long is Anthony staying in Calcutta, could this be the last time she sees him, his eyes are upon her, she decides it will be within the confines of polite conversation if she asks him, how long are you planning to stay in Calcutta? He laughs, quite a long time I should think, as long as it takes.

They take the tram back, she and her brother, I think the saheb has taken a fancy to you, he jokes. The amusement in his voice depresses her, is that all these two afternoons are to be reduced to, a joke for the theater group, for Anthony an amusing tropical memory. She is determined that, although nothing can possibly happen between them, she will sear her memory upon him, like the girl in a white dress on the Coney Island ferry in the film she has just seen, perhaps before he dies, like Charles Foster Kane, he will whisper, "Moni."

Perhaps, before he dies, he will whisper, "Moni," or perhaps the name of their child, for he will never see them again, not after Monday morning. He will come back to a dark hallway, dark rooms where the paper chains he will have put up the night before sway miserably, empty rooms, balloons floating against the walls, a party that has not been, sadder even than a party that is over.

The child calls for her. She gathers her into her arms and rocks her gently. What sort of cake will I have? the girl asks for the millionth time. A rabbit cake, she answers, and she has to draw a rabbit cake for her, with her stubby crayons, a rabbit cake with six bright candles. Years ago, her cousins would beg her to draw diagrams for them in their exercise books, the innards of a frog, roots and tubers, vernier calipers, a world she knew nothing of. Some of the strange words worked a curious enchantment within her, she could not shake them off, sinus venosus, part of a frog's heart, she remembers, she was particularly fascinated with, the more she tried to forget its ruthless cadence, the more it would come back to haunt her, until utterly exhausted on the bus home, she would submit to its absurd rhythm, let it take over her mind, sinus venosus.

The child is asleep now, wrapped around a teddy bear, the autumn evening is imbued with a penetrating silence, that for her is the welcome quiet before a long awaited storm. She sits for a long time, by the child's bed, absorbing the darkness, it is after many years, it seems, that she can sense the texture of darkness, darkness, friend of her childhood, who played hide-and-seek with her under wintertime quilts, darkness, her first lover, engulfing her in secret embrace, grainy kisses upon her burning lips, darkness, her accomplice, in their mossy bathroom, soothing her tender limbs, flowing between her quivering thighs, darkness, who had followed her from her native land in the eyes of a madman playing "Greensleeves" at Warren Street Station from the hollow of a beggar's hand stretched out across a baked tropical pavement, to be rinsed out in the gray of a sleepless dawn, she had battled with darkness, darkness had become an indifferent enemy. On this autumn evening, her child's cheek upon her hand, she makes peace with darkness, and after she has lightly shut the bedroom door, darkness, an old lover, seizes her again from behind, enfolds her in desperate embrace, his fingers stream across her hair, her arms, her breasts, on the shadowed landing, she commits adultery with darkness. And afterwards, she sits on the stairs, among the grotesque shadows of the stuffed animals, the darkness around her is sparse and brittle, she longs for the dense buttery dark of a moonless tropical night, like that which hid from her Anthony's face, on their wedding night when she had submitted to his undammed lust, the running tide of his desire, when with horror and relief she had let his violent lips roam her body, darkness had masked her fragile agony as he thrust desperately into her, darkness had stood by, betrayed. Later as he slept, his face in her hair, she had opened her wet thighs to darkness, to wash away her burning, to cleanse her. She cannot sleep, and as she stares into the thick blackness, it begins to fade, a dull dawn smears the walls of the whitewashed room, a rented room, in a rented house, a house rented for the wedding, in this very bed, tonight, some other shy couple will explore each other, perhaps they will never have met before, or sat across from each other, only a few times, in an awkward silence, watched by smiling relatives. The day before, she had been made to wake before sunrise and eat her last meal as a virgin, and then she had fasted until after the ceremony, and afterwards she had played dazedly with her food, eating little, and now a painful acidity rose within her, she longed for cool yogurt. She watched the gray light upon Anthony's broad, bare back, she had imagined often, on noisy tropical mornings, pretending to be asleep with her head buried in her pillow, what it would be like to wake beside a man, she imagined a distant rural mansion, an old feudal palace, a bed beside a window overlooking a river, she would sit up to watch the boats, hear the distant strains of a fisherman's song, he would watch her, his hands behind his head, elbows out, that was the shape of her girlhood dream, fashioned amid the clatter of the milk pails, the bellowing of the roadside cows, the incomprehensible shrieks of the early-morning vendors, a harsh lemon sunlight forcing through the closed shutters. Hunger gnaws at her, outside in the mild winter light, large vats of food are rotting, mounds of pilau rice, piles of fried fish, caldrons of oily meat, boxes of sweetmeats, the excess from last night's feast, they will flow in rivers through the drains of Calcutta. If she had married a Bengali, one of the quiet youths, perhaps, from the theater group that had run around so furiously the day before, helping with the last-minute arrangements, if she had, as her brother had surely hoped, married one of them, she has a feeling that there would never have been such a wedding, that her brother would never have stood for it, that the young man she might have married would never have stood for it, for they despised all ritualistic excess, or perhaps they would have given in, but not without protest, not with the bitter sympathy that her brother had accepted this one absurd request of his grief-stricken father. And now, she will go back to them, bring to them a new grief, that of a daughter returned, a daughter rejected, a daughter spurned.

She makes her way down the stairs in the insubstantial darkness that has, once again, become remote, and follows the hallway to the kitchen, where for the first time that evening, she switches on a light. She must eat something, although her excitement is sustenance enough. She opens the fridge, bottles of milk line the door, milk she has put aside to make sweets for the party, Indian sweets, she will make them, she will make them now. She sets the milk to boil in a large pan, and makes some toast. Will she miss the technology, the creature comforts that were the bane of so many patriotic souls, the microwave oven, the washing machine, the electric kettle, she surveys her gadgets as she eats her toast, will she miss them, will she miss the food, the fresh bread, the undiluted milk, Scottish marmalade, diet mayonnaise, polyunsaturated margarine, they had said on TV the other day that polyunsaturates were worse for you than whatever they had replaced, and Anna and Anthony had found this horribly amusing, never trusted polywhatsernames anyway, Anna had said, crying with laughter. The milk is beginning to boil, she pours in lemon juice, and stirs, the milk begins to curdle, like baby vomit, she will strain it through a clean cloth and hang it for hours to dry. And then she will knead it with sugar, and fashion from it little circles and diamonds, and garnish each with a raisin, sweets that will lie, uneaten, upon the dining table, together with the bunny-rabbit cake, the mounds of sandwiches, the jelly oranges, pork pies, the jam tarts and sausage rolls, food that will go to waste like the vast excesses

from her wedding feast that festered outside as she lay, numb
with hunger, trapped against his bare back on their nuptial bed.
And in the cruel cold dawn he had shivered and woken, reached
for the silk punjabi shirt that he had been made to wear through
the ceremony, his chin smeared with vermilion from her head,
and she had said to him, I am so very hungry, I just cannot sleep,
and he had replied that lovemaking made one hungry, and for
the first time, like the slap of wet fish, the realization that he had
made love to many many other women came down upon her,
and yet she wondered why she had not come to terms with this
obvious fact before, why had she assumed that those deep eyes
had never hungered for anyone but her, that those large quiet
hands had never before trembled with such passion, why was it
only in the act of love that it had become clear that there had
been many others before her, why did the strange silence of
fulfilled desire carry the hint that there would be many more
after? His lust has a different language with Anna, she knows
that often she forms the cornerstone in the choreography of their
passion, that it is for Anna's benefit that he will often stroke with
gentle madness her own forest of hair, she plays a silent role in
their intricate foreplay, and the unbearable sadness of their
dead love is what sustains his wide desire. Theirs had been a
sweet and shallow desire, she admits to herself, stirring the
curdled milk, a desire that should have been allowed to die with
the last rays of the evening sun, a desire that should have remained a bittersweet tropical memory, and come back to haunt
them in the peace of their old age, to cloud their tired eyes with
memories of a more tender, pure passion than that which they
would have built their lives upon, one that could never be.

She hears the key turn in the lock, and for one frozen moment
she is petrifed that her new mood, smooth as an eggshell, will
crumble under the weight of his presence. She can see in the
hallway his firm shoulders move as he hangs up his coat, she is

paralyzed by a forgotten desire that makes her flinch when he lays his broad hands upon her arms, the smell of another woman thick on his fingertips, in the ice of his lips upon her cheek, his satiated smile.

Sweets for the party? He kisses her head. He pulls out a stool and sits down, Anna will pick her up at ten tomorrow, he says, there is a childish eagerness in his voice, perhaps the sweet anticipation of a party is what their love will feed on, over this weekend, or is it merely the vast memory of his own childhood parties, the interminable wait for the clean cold smell of a birthday among your bedsheets as you wake, a birthday breakfast, brimming with excitement, birthday kisses, at school your name is announced at assembly, eyes turn to you, the smug, grateful eyes of those you have invited to your party, the forlorn looks of those you have neglected, you lower your head and smile, lessons drag, but you are in a dream, words hang suspended in your rarefied consciousness, it is your birthday, and at home the deep smell of long hours of baking, the decorations sway impatiently, waiting, waiting, and the ghost of this excitement will stay with you forever as will the ghost of its forlorn dregs, the shattered balloons, the twisted straws, the colored paper in crumpled heaps, for many years, as you clear away the empty glasses, swab the alcohol from the carpet, that strange void will engulf you from time to time, the ancestor of a presentiment of death.

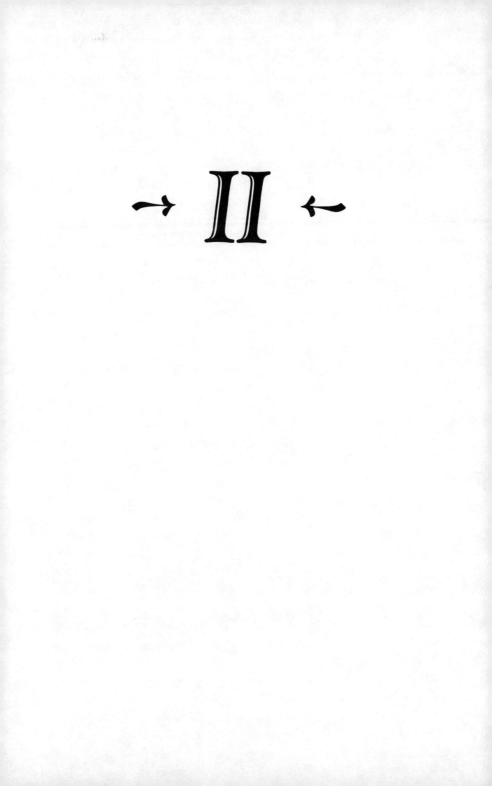

Saturday morning, the sweet thud of letters crashing on the wooden floor breaks his satisfied sleep, he lies back for a while and allows the morning to sediment within him, screams of horror and delight from the bathroom tell him that she is bathing the child, soaping with cruel calmness those shivering limbs, tortured curls under the Pink Panther towel, and finally the warmth of hair dryer, warm clothes picked off the radiator, a proud bow in her hair, she is ready to go shopping with Anna, she runs in to kiss him before she leaves. He can feel Anna's presence within the house, his home, his castle, a king among his bedsheets, he lies quietly and listens to her hard footsteps in the hallway, the swish of her skirts against the banister, he is overcome, once again, by the intellectual comfort of their existence, the symmetry of their being, and yet, how would they grow old, he wonders, one day, surely, he would lose her, they would lose her, he and Moni, someday, Anna would marry some brash young artist, and they would return from the wedding, feeling old and withered, and sit in the dark, bent with sorrow, but on that day too, he would find some way to take comfort in his sorrow, the beauty of parting would engulf him in its delicious poison. Many years ago, in Calcutta, he had awaited this emotion, the sweet sorrow of sad parting, in the shade of the palm trees, on Amrita's veranda, he had courted this sorrow, and instead the thought of being apart from those bright black eyes had gathered like a monsoon gloom within his veins. It had become clear to him then, amid the dim glow of the asynchronous streetlights, the incessant blare of car horns that rent the smoky autumn evening, it had become clear to him then that he could not leave this putrefying city without her, that it would not be enough to cherish the beauty of their unconsummated passion, alongside his memories of this unashamed city, its gorged pavements, the tired faces of colonial buildings jostled by indifferent, insect-eyed multistoried flats, the patient streets lacerated by the construction of an underground, the smell of hot mud after a brief rain. That evening, as he sat with the theater group, outside Max Mueller Bhavan, the German cultural center, he was astonished by a sudden sense of awe that descended upon him as he watched the careless movements of her brother, waving his vile cigarette, as he argued with two of the other men about German expressionism, they talked fast, mainly in English, often for his benefit, although he had noticed even when they discussed something amongst themselves they used English lavishly, and today, although they tried to draw him in, he felt utterly excluded, he was an alien, and suddenly he was no longer content to be a detached observer, the gentle anthropologist, it was a role that had become bitter to him. For one bleak instant, as he dissolved sterilizing iodine in his lassi, he felt a wistful urge to be part of them, the forgotten anguish of childhood ostracism, the torture of a new school, waiting quietly to be accepted, the chill of chipped inkwells seeps into his fingers as lunchtime approaches, where can he sit among the vast sea of unfamiliar faces? And then, she is there, swinging her cloth bag, she sits across from him, takes off a worn high-heeled shoe and rubs a small well-formed foot, I walked all the way from Park Street, she tells them, smiling, the buses are impossible, she looks at him, her eyes are shining, did you come straight from your French class then, Amrita asks her. Small green insects swarm insanely to-ward the light above his head, he picks one off his shirt, we call those after the Goddess Kali, her brother tells him, they always appear at this time of the year, near the day that we light fireworks to worship her, which is, as you know, tomorrow. He has invited Anthony to spend the evening at their house, to witness the pyrotechnics, the homemade fireworks that their cousins had crafted out of gunpowder and clay, the store-bought crackers, toffee-shaped "chocolate bombs," wilting rockets, inebriated catherine wheels. In the park outside their home, the set of serene idols that graced a large canopy during the three days of puja festivities, a few weeks ago, has been replaced by the charred figure of Kali, Goddess of Destruction, alter ego of the bleached lion-borne Durga, who had stood there in her place just a few weeks ago, surrounded by her family, her daughters— the Goddess of Learning astride a swan, the Goddess of Wealth borne on an owl, and her sons—the elephant-headed Ganesh, the effete Warrior God, Kartik, whose wife, Moni had explained to him in her cautious English, was a banana tree, and her brother had cut in to tell him, amid the din of the drums and loudspeakers blaring popular film music, her brother had yelled indignantly into his ear that the traditional images were never so serene, that these idols had been modeled after the popular film stars, thus religion and popular cinema had achieved an ironic synergy. There had been no such compromise with Kali though, her flaming tongue hung in shame over her garland of human heads, shame at having laid her feet upon her husband, the lord Shiva, who was always reduced to a black phallus, a smooth dark stone in household shrines, he had watched Amrita's mother-in-law in her vast room of worship bathe and daub it with sandalwood paste, along with her other little figurines, her photographs of holy men.

He watched the sky darken, that evening, as the city prepared to worship the fearful Kali, he watched the sky fade over Max

Mueller Bhavan, with a feeling of despair, the cold thought that she who sat before him in the harsh lamplight could never be possessed, even if her eyes spoke of an unknown tenderness, and sometimes were shadowed with the terror of the dim awakening of a first lust, and even if her shoulders quaked when he steadied her on a rocky bus ride, even if her ears flamed as he drew near to speak above the festival din, even so, he had never really held her hands, they had never spoken of their emotions except in oblique playful phrases, how could he tell her that, for him, the game was over, what was the language of love in this world? He had come to this land, as his forefathers had done, with a conviction that all he wanted would be his, he had not come with greed, only a desire for knowledge, for experience, and he had known that these would be there for him, and so far he had enjoyed their unspoken romance, secure in his belief that he would never want of her any more than she was prepared to give. Now, he watched her, gulping her lassi, struggling to put on her shoe with the free hand, the lips came away, yogurt-rimmed, the desire to kiss them burned terribly within him, a deep gloom shrouded his eyes. In the auditorium he makes no attempt to sit beside her, takes comfort in the worried glance she casts at him from the other end of the row, some of the group members suppress a smile, it is a joke to them, his impossible infatuation, and until he had realized its gravity, it had, in some strange way, been of some amusement to him, too. His gloom deepens, when after the performance, they sit and tear to shreds the crude attempts of the dancer to synthesize Eastern and Western modes, her eyes are upon him, the beginnings of a smile flutter upon her lips as she implores him to respond, and then suddenly, she gives up, ignores him for the rest of the evening, he watches her as she climbs onto her brother's motorbike, her sari billows in the darkness as they pass by, he follows Amrita and her husband, who had arrived late for the recital, and slept in his business suit on the seat beside him through the entire second half, he follows them to their car, inhales the bitter night smoke of a thousand clay ovens on the short ride home. Amrita and her husband have a wedding to attend, so they drop him off, we won't stay long, she assures him, that's why we're going so late, he walks down the gravel driveway to the portico, a servant stands with the door open. Inside, Amrita's mother-in-law is waiting up with food for him, warm puffed bread and mutton curry, she will sit with him at the marble dining table directing the servants, and speaking, in her colonial English, of her trips to Europe and America, in days gone before, he has always listened with amusement and interest, tonight they have a soothing effect on him, her proud and wistful anecdotes of a postwar England, there she had, in some stately hotel off Oxford Street, brought into the world, a week before he was due, her only son, the man that, inexplicably, Amrita had married, a quiet gentleman, an executive in some chemical company, he did not share his wife's attachment to the arts but donated large sums of money to the theater group, after dinner Anthony wanders into his den, a small room where he works on the weekends, and where he reads in the evenings, the shelves are stacked with science fiction novels and detective stories, he searches among them for something to read in bed, for he fears he will not be able to sleep. Indeed, as he turns the last page, a sickening gray dawn is trickling in, a sad crow perches on the sill, he has a feeling that somewhere within this grave city, she, too, is staring into the first morbid light of the day, and that although nothing has passed between them except the impalpable caress of their eyes, their love has been nourished by their silence, she, too, must feel the agony of immured passion.

He woke, late in the day, to a clear, soft blue sky, in the air an inexplicable sweetness, the mature lust of a tropical autumn, he spent the afternoon reading in the garden, and when the sun began to dip in the gentle sky, he asked the driver to drop him off near Moni's house. He walked through the park, swinging a box of cakes, the first sparklers are shining in the faded light, the first futile crackers. A grand excitement pervades their household, all doors are open, the neighbors from upstairs crowd onto their veranda, trays of fireworks lie on the living-room floor, children dart back and forth, brandishing sparklers, lines of candles adorn the windows, she is lighting them, one by one. He moves towards her, can I help, he asks, and takes from her trembling fingers a box of matches, they light them together, in silence, the dusk between them thick with passion, the fragrance of molten wax. Every house in the city is lit with streams of candles, perhaps she can take him up to the roof terrace to see this grand effect, yes, the roof, she mumbles, confused, and amid the commotion, they slip away, up the musty stairs, onto the dark roof. Indeed, the city is ablaze, with candles in every window, rockets shoot up into the clear darkness, the roar of crackers vies with the loudspeakers in the park, and downstairs her cousins are igniting the round clay fireworks that they have baked themselves, they rotate the lit ball in their bare hands, and fling it with a flourish to the heavens where it bursts into a geyser of sparks. There, on the darkened rooftop, amid the thunder of the festival of fire, the smell of gunpowder in the air, he reaches out, for the first time, to take into his feverish hands her floury fingers, she has been rolling dough, all afternoon, he engulfs her in sudden embrace, runs his anguished hands through her hair, kisses a burning cheek, and although she is stiff in his arms, in her silence there is response, the heaviness of her breath, the pounding of her heart, but she draws back quickly as some children burst through the doors, chasing each other with their sparklers. One of the girls stops and offers them a sparkler each, which she lights with her own, and then they are alone again, he draws her behind the water tank, lifts her face to the incendiary skies, sparks shower onto her hair, he kisses the frightened lips, she breaks away, she says, she will be missed downstairs, why don't you stay here, I will come up when I can. She moves quickly into the shadows, the sparkler hanging limply from one hand. He runs his tongue across his lips, tastes grains of flour. When she returns, half an hour later, a plate of food in her hand, her brother is there, explaining in absurd detail how the fireworks are made. Later, he watches her, down below, on the street, lighting rockets, diminutive catherine wheels, for the children that crowd around her. He will not hold her again until the night of their wedding, in the months to come their hands will be their only instruments of love, in the dark of theater halls, under table covers, in the black-and-yellow Calcutta cabs with his nails digging into her palms he will declare his desperate love, she will answer with tremulous silence, and when he tells her she must come back with him, she will shake her head, slow tears will travel across her cheeks, lose themselves in the corners of her smile.

In the air today, this fresh Saturday morning, there is a hint of that palpable tropical festivity that he inhaled, ten years ago, in Calcutta, during those autumn months, the bamboo skeletons of the marquees against a washed sky, the unfinished figures of the gods in the potters' quarters flourishing their unadorned limbs, the streets tense with frantic shoppers, the reek of excitement that had shielded and nurtured their love. He emerges from his cocoon of bedsheets, and makes his way downstairs, she is watching television, he pours himself some coffee and takes up the newspaper. It does not please him that she is so languid, so inactive, there seems to be a strange sadness upon her face, one that is devoid of the beauty of her loneliness, of the silent nights she waits for him to come back from reckless love-making, there is a tired indifference in those eyes that eats into his peace, his festive mood. He puts down his paper and looks across at her, unshaven, dark eyes in sleep-soothed hollows, and as she is hit by the remembrance of the intensity of her love for him, he says to her, perhaps you should go home for some time, you look so tired, Anna and I can take care of the child.

She sips her cold, bitter coffee, silent. A chill anger froths within her, she realizes that although his rejection is slow and gentle, it is definite, if she does not fit into his scheme, she may as well be gone.

You think I am trying to get rid of you, he says sadly, repentant, but I love you, I want you here, but I want you to be happy, I want us all to be happy.

Why should she not be happy? The sadness of his infidelity should not cripple her, she no longer feels any attraction for him, this he is painfully aware of, she has his trust, his respect, his affectionate devotion. She has a job, translating the complaints of Bangladeshi patients to physicians, she has a life, she has a daughter, what more could life have offered her, there, behind decayed shutters, from where he had rescued her, a more faithful marriage perhaps, but then she had loved him, would she have been able to forget him, there against the somber skies, would she have made a bonfire of her emotions, there among the diseased fields, it was she that had submitted to him, smelling of flour and gunpowder, to be scarred forever, if he had not taken command of her life then, her underdeveloped mind, watered by Romantic poetry, would have withered, she would never have recovered from his love, if he had abandoned her, then. What would have been her fate, tainted by his merciless passion, would she have resisted marriage, surrendering finally to some prearranged match out of sheer loneliness, some unknown customer of her body, she would remain, a timid teacher of English in some girls' school, mother of two, on humid holiday afternoons she would dust her brass knickknacks, her framed portrait of Tagore, teach her children how to sing, and on some unpleasant evenings, the children would peep from the bedroom door to see her standing in tears, as her husband firmly wheeled her drunken brother out of the door. Perhaps, on some summer day, she would laugh with some college friend about the Englishman who had obsessed her for so many years, perhaps, in the cool of closed shutters, on a languorous summer afternoon, while the household slept, she and her friend would lie and talk of him, and she would recount in passionate detail how he had once touched her, kissed her upon her lips, in the shadow of the water tank, the chorus of firecrackers, the quiet thunder of his lips on her hair, as her friend drifts into sleep, she would lie and remember, her coarsened hands would tremble upon a mature bosom, he had saved her from such a sterile existence, from the disaster of a secure and meaningless life, he had kissed the wax between her turmeric-stained fingers, on that night of fire and thunder, in the shadow of the water tank, he had crowned her with sparks.

He had given her the world, the countless trips to Europe, would she ever have seen France, but for him, home to the language she had worshiped, studied so devoutly at the Calcutta Alliance Française, would she have known to drink the right wines, the cheeses that she had longed to taste, that strange rhythmic catalogue in her Beginner's French text, Camembert, Livarot, Roquefort, Roblochon, Brie, he remembers her profound awe at the first menacing glimpse of the Alps, he had seen her move, as in a dream through the Louvre, in Venice, she had stepped out of the train, and breathing deeply of the rotten canals she had said with simple wonder, so I have seen Venice, all this and much more he had given to her, stood back the enchanted benefactor, a lover that is confident he can please his beloved, and he had reveled in the purity of her joy, dreams he had helped realize, and it was on such a trip to the hills of Provence, accompanied by his old friend Trevor and Trevor's young girlfriend Anna, it was on such a trip, that he had come back to her, his lips stained with the sweetness of another woman, on a night of warm lavender and pale wind, he had walked across the moonlit pebbles intoxicated by a much fuller lust than she had ever seeded within him, made savage, selfish love to her so that she had longed for the burning wind to cauterize her sorrow, to incinerate his guilt, the burning wind that had she had read of, many years ago, her back against a chalky wall, by murky monsoon light, she had read of a burning wind that drove the artist insane, and that night, staring into the smooth olive blackness, she had wished that instead of the fragrant breezes that lapped against her, there be a mordant wind.

He cannot bear her sorrow, it is the sorrow of a dying bird he has catapulted down, fluttering in his palm, the incredulous grief of an abandoned pet, he takes a small, cold hand into his, he says, smiling, do you remember our first trip to Paris?

Did she remember, huddled in the tiny, damp flat in this unfriendly city, deeply homesick, did she remember, he appears, hunched in his old overcoat, guess where we are going, tonight? The train rushing through the dark, he sleeps against her shoulder, long legs folded up against the seat across, and the first smell of the dull English sea, and then at dawn, they are there, their first trip to Paris, a cheap hotel in the Latin Quarter, she sits in a daze upon the concave bed as he shaves, that mysterious object is not a loo, he explains, but a bidet, the bathroom, out on the landing, she refuses to use, she prefers to wait to use the toilets at a restaurant, at an exhibition, and that afternoon, she peers through the glass at the *Mona Lisa,* her hands clenched around his, tears in her eyes for her brother, suffused with guilt that he who introduced her to this world sits proofreading newspaper articles, many miles away, while she is here, face to face with the smile, the smile that he had cut out of some advertisement and pasted across the wall above his alcove where his desk was kept, so many mornings she has emerged from the bathroom, toweling her hair, and her eyes have traveled from the sharp shoulder blades moving furiously against the skin of his back, the greasy head, bent low, and above, on the cracked wall, between a photograph of his favorite filmmaker, Mrinal Sen, and a badly typed American Indian poem, the smile. That night, she threw up their French meal, their one extravagance, all over the orange basin in their room, they worried that she might be pregnant, he told her he would get a job, somehow, soon, sitting on the steps of Montmartre listening to pavement musicians playing Beatles songs, she is seized by a desire to stay forever, never to return to cruel London, the stacks of index cards on the blue carpet, the cold metal of the typewriter under her dust-cloth, the thesis he would never finish. She does not want to return to the smoky pubs, the evenings with his friends that talk so fast, spill her chicken curry and their beer onto the Kashmiri rug that was Sharmila's wedding present to her, the evenings that they spend alone, the hollow click of his typewriter in the damp silence, but there were nights then, when they had sat together and laughed and talked, and yet even then, within themselves there had been a strange nostalgia, as if they had already begun to live on the memory of their love.

On this autumn morning, two days before she will leave him, she masks the agony and indecision she has nursed through the dawn, with a slow smile. He tweaks her cheek, I still think you should go, he says, you really need a change, we will go and fetch you at Christmas, I would like to go myself, he wonders what it will be like, to wander down the same streets that he walked upon, delirious with love for her, how would they feel, walking by restaurants where his hands had groped under the dark of the table for her nervous fingers, the forlorn fields where they had sat and watched cricket, on bright winter days before their wedding, we will come at Christmas he tells her, to bring you back.

As she cracks eggs in the kitchen, she muses bitterly, whether by "we" he meant just himself and the child, or was he thinking of bringing Anna to trespass upon the territory of their memories, the sacred streets, the clean circles of dung patties against the honest winter skies. The sense of absurdity that has been gnawing her all morning, the unnecessary drama of her plan, once again, becomes a source of an inexplicable pleasure,

on this dark and lonely path, doom has befriended me

the egg yolks fall, shiny and cold into the glass bowl, she can hear him bathing upstairs, preening himself for his lover, this new bitterness rubs within her like coarse grains of sand, a desiccated moth wing lands gently on the lake of yolk. Six years ago, motherhood had enveloped her in a tender numbness, the warm heaviness of milk in her breasts, sleepless nights and swollen mornings, redolent of ripe flowers, that sweet narcosis is finally dripping away, leaving her mind clear, and calm, like ice.

Among the ashen butterflies of the Ardèche, she had felt the first soft nausea of maternity smother the chill fear within her that he would leave her for the tall girl with green eyes, who held him in her deep green gaze like a shore pebble within stiff sea foam, whose limbs moved like music in the stale sunlight, whose hair hung like webs of silk in the soft wind, and the deep languor of the months that followed had eased the agony of his penitent hands upon her, evenings that he had watched over her torpid form with broken eyes, bathed her heavy ankles with herbal salts, and kissed with penetrating sadness, her swollen fingers, she had been immune in her new numbness to his indecision, the slow heartbeats of the child within her had obscured his tension, the gentle swish of her blood, and a persistent memory of the aroma of naphthalene overwhelmed the foreign smell upon his flesh, her mouth, choked with moths, did not taste her juices upon his bruised lips, her thoughts coursed thinly through her consciousness like the veiny desiccation of ivy on old church walls.

She remembers the first time Anna came to see the child, she lay helpless, numb against the pillows, while he held the baby up to her, a placid, wrinkled bird in his broad hands, the green of her eyes had deepened with lust like a cloud shadow creeping upon the sea, his fatherhood excited her. Yet her own disquiet as she watched Anna trace, with a trembling finger, the soft lines upon her child's cheek, the dull ache had lulled her into a dense cloudy slumber, where the memory of his first, impalpable treason stood like a shadow of pain, far far away, that evening, long before he met Anna, when, for the first time, his eyes had strayed to the caressing hazel glances of an American college girl they met at a party, the bitter night that followed, the first intangible deceit, the first violation of those sacred vows, whispered in Sanskrit by a croaky Brahmin on a cold Calcutta evening, fire had stood witness to their union then, and darkness watched them now as they came to terms with its silent dissolution, that first night of pain as she felt his faltering lips upon her, seeking for some other flesh, his guilty eyes at breakfast, roving the space beyond her, the unbearable torture of the hours that he spent listening over and over again to the *German Requiem* in the living room, when every time she entered she felt an intruder to his anguish, a Saturday afternoon, and suddenly, with the twilight comes a sacred repentance, a new confidence in their love, he is hers alone, they drive out to his mother's in Bristol, and that was how it had ended, that first torment, harsh hollow pain, it had almost purified their love, convinced him that marriage was not an obsession but a refuge from obsession, and from then on, his heart had roamed, only to come back, every time, fresher, reassured that the love that he felt for her was not of this world,

I lose you, my beloved, so that I may rediscover you
Though oft immersed in a tide of some other enchantment
You remain invisible, yet you are not of the shadows.
I seek you, my mind trembles with fear, waves terrify my passion
You conceal your boundlessness under a cloak of void
But my grief washes away the mirth of that deception.

The impermanence of his many obsessions hung bittersweet around her, as she watched him gravitate inexorably towards the grass green of Anna's eyes. They returned like old mosquito bites, the memories of his intermittent infatuations, the sharp stab of the first amorous glances, the humiliation of his slow, sensual smile flung across the room at some defiant gaze, the mild itch of these memories masked the horror of his final passion, one from which he would not return, I lose you my beloved, and you will remain among the shadows that will be my world, a strange haze of warmth, of compassion, a memory of pain.

She pours herself a mug of coffee, the drug that has sealed her impermeability to the world, coffee, the dark torture of the condensed bitterness knit against her tongue, a petrified excitement, coffee had been her deliverance when the torpor of childbirth began to drip away, coffee-making offered a strange sexuality, the sensual aroma of crushed beans, beans, smooth and voluptuous, overflowing in her palms, and later, the soiled filters, the murky residue of a spent lust.

He appears in the doorway, dark, wet hair swept off his tall furrowed forehead, those ridges that she has swept with her lips, kissed his pale lids, asleep in a sea of index cards, she had crept away to her job at the public library, and in the afternoon, she would return to an empty flat, the remains of his cold lunch next to the typewriter, she would watch television until it was time to cook, and sometimes he would come back with Trevor, and she would have to make potato curry to stretch out the meal among the three of them, and perhaps as they talked, she would fall asleep watching a television film, or settle into a peaceful slumber while reading in bed, he might come in to tell her they were going down to the pub, and later he would wake her up to make love, smelling of India Pale Ale and typewriter carbon. And then he would type, late into the night, wearing his over-coat until the heat came on again at dawn, and sometimes, he would fall asleep, pillowed by his papers, and that was how she might find him, hold his rough chin in her hands, inhale the fermented odor of his troublesome dreams, and some afternoons she would return to a ravaged silence, an immense frustration that lay like a distant sea within him, she did not dare then to lay her quiet hands upon his brow.

He lays a cool, clean-shaven cheek against hers, stinging of anticipation, he is waiting for them to return, Anna and their child, a broad smile pushes against her chin, should I take Mon-day off? he asks.

For a moment she is frozen with fear, it dawns upon her that her plan is terribly fragile, her own indecision is not her only enemy, that she may indeed still be here on Monday evening, suitcases packed in the closets upstairs, she may be here, wretched in the failure of her plan, she is on the shores of a deep misery, a long-lasting despair, if her plan fails, she will be left to drown, the dull slow destruction of her consciousness will con-tinue, they will remain suspended in the stale winds of their unresolved conflict, if she cannot submit to the sweet doom of departure, she may be here, on Monday evening, clearing the remains of the birthday party with bitter fingers, the colors of the crepe paper will bleed under her futile tears.

The doorbell rings, they are back, she melts butter in the frying pan, the child rushes in, her arms full, she lifts her eyes from the swirling butter, they travel down the hallway, where his broad back obscures the looks of love that they are exchanging, the complicity of their mingled breath falls as mist against the panes of frosted glass, his hands hang clenched with passion at his side, the acrid smell of burning butter fills the air.

As she tips out the charred liquid into the sink, she can hear the slow swish of Anna's skirts as she pushes past him and walks down the hall to the kitchen,

"Have you shown your mother the dress?" Anna asks the child. "It's a bit on the large side," she explains to Moni. "Mother can take it in for her, this afternoon. You are coming to tea, aren't you? I'll help with anything you have to do for the party."

Her hand trembles as she slides a fresh pat of butter into the pan, she thinks of the kind, old woman in her large, lonely house, Anna's mother, many summer evenings they have sat out in her garden eating prawn sandwiches, they are memories of a deep peace, the veiny legs of the old woman tucked together under a garden chair, the child upon her lap, Anthony lies upon the sweet summer grass with his head in her lap, his eyes upon Anna as she twists wild flowers into long chains with which she crowns the child. On such evenings, the low click of golf balls in the distance, he has buried his hungry breath in the sun-warmed folds of her cotton sari, the child has drifted into sleep to a summer tale of rabbits and beavers that Anna reads from a book she has selected from the shelves that line the little room upstairs where she spent her childhood, the summers back from boarding school, where, upon the old wooden floor, one winter evening, many years ago, he and Anna had made love for the first time, having driven madly through the rain, all afternoon, consumed by desire, they had driven aimlessly through the pouring rain, until Anna had remarked that they were close to her mother's house, her mother was away, he had kissed her ice-cold hands as she fumbled with the keys, they stood dripping in the tall, musty hallway, in the cloakroom he noticed a plaque, the ten commandments of golf, thou shalt not hold the sport second to thy spouse, she stood in the landing, staring out at the rain, he ran up to her, wrung her damp hair in his hands, the intoxicating rain steam that rose from her breasts, she led him upstairs, flung open the door to her room, this is where I spent my childhood, she whispered, her early paintings hang on the walls, figures of dancers, my sister was my first model, she told him, she pulled aside the heavy curtains, he drew his fingers down the dusty spine of *Wuthering Heights*, what are we to do? she asked him. I cannot leave her, ever, he told her, as she knelt beside him, I cannot leave her, he mumbled as he moved his lips upon her damp neck, and as if these words excited her, she drew him upon the hard wooden floor, kicked away at the rugs, and there for the first time he made love to her, against the cold, pitted wood, and later he had sat across from his mother at his home, rubbing his bruised knees, while his wife slept upstairs, his mother had glanced suspiciously across, over her knitting, as he ran his fingers over his sore knees, how can you stay out so late while she is in this condition, she accused him, there, that's done, she flattened out a small bootie, he watched, fascinated. That was the only time they had made love in that stately house, they returned many times, Anna's mother doted upon the baby, there have been many summer evenings, Moni remembers, in the pale darkness, she has fancied an aroma of roasting mosquitoes, as intermittent crackles issued from a new mosquito-trapping device, one that drew them inexorably, by means of some mysterious hum, into its infernal confines. She will miss the old lady, the peculiar grain of her voice, the gentle hands weighed down by heavy rings, the fragile perfume of a forgotten era that surrounds her always, a smell of rich flowers, she touches everything with a delicate firmness, a stalk of celery, a lace doily, the child's fine hair falls through her wrinkled fingers, she has the magnanimous confidence of one who has lived with beauty all her life, there has been an unusual comfort in watching her arrange parsley on their dinner plates, as Anna and Anthony sit wrapped in their passion, listening to music in the library, Moni has allowed the clean symmetry of the sprigs of parsley upon white china to permeate her mind, she has found peace in the quiet rhythm of fingers gently spreading the green stalks.

She covers the mushrooms and leans back against the counter, the coffee has lost its warmth, a fan of cold bitterness spread out in her mouth, she has spent so much of her time in this house against this counter, the sharp edge of formica cutting into the loose flesh of her belly, still relaxed from childbirth, she has filled her hours with the mindless creation of food, the shelf across is crammed with cookery books, scraps of hasty recipes are impaled upon a corkboard, but it had never become an art to her, never afforded her the sense of fulfillment, the pleasure was in the mechanical precision, in surrendering your mind to the definite instructions, chop the onions, dice the chicken, stir for three minutes and add five tablespoons of butter, it aggravated her when the instructions were not exact, when recipes called for a "packet" of yeast, a "pinch" of salt, a "thumb" of ginger, she had surrounded herself with scales and measures, with graduated glass containers, enemies of imagination, props for her apathy.

Anna has gone upstairs with the child to help her with the new dress, Anthony stands in the doorway to the kitchen, absorbing the sounds of laughter, the few shrieks that drift down from above, a murky, formless anger rises within her, she will leave him, but will it be enough to merely envisage the depths of his despair, as he presses furiously on the doorbell, on Monday afternoon, confused, reaches for his keys inside his Gladstone bag, opens the door to an iced silence, how can she be sure that as he sits among the futile decorations, his tears will not be diluted with relief, that he will not take Anna's hand and press it to his burning forehead, that he will not draw her down among the floating balloons and the limp paper chains, to make love, that their new grief will not bind them closer, nourish their complex passion, how will she know, if she is not there, if she cannot observe, silent, from a corner, the disintegration of his world, she would like to wipe the complacent smile from his lips with her own tortured fingers, kiss his acid tears with cold, coffee-stained lips, instead she will be far away, rushing towards darkness with her arms around a confused child, returning to the land where he found her, many years ago, on a night when the skies vomited rain, in the festering darkness, he had thirsted for her eyes.

Many years ago, he had listened for the sounds of her movement behind the curtains that shielded the rest of the house from their living room, for the soft sounds of her bare feet, the clink of her bracelets, these beloved signs of her existence within, he had listened with more impatience than today, with his head against the doorframe, he takes in the sounds of the frolic upstairs. He would appear sometimes, in the morning, as she prepared herself for college, he would sit on a chair drinking coffee, conversing with her unwashed brother, as she gulped down weak fish curry, steaming upon her plate, trying to leaf through, for the last time before a class test, some curry-stained, dog-eared text, while her grandmother tried to tame with a lurid comb her unruly wet tresses, his smiling eyes would drift towards her, and later as she struggled with her shoes in her hurry to be off, he would offer her a ride in a taxi, since he, too, was going towards the city center, and upon Rashbehari Avenue, he would watch with desperate desire the lips that she bit in frustration and anxiety, as taxi after taxi passed with its meter down, and often they would be forced to push their way into some overflowing bus, and yet the pressure of his body against hers became anonymous within the tide of humanity that bore upon them, pushed them apart, so that he would only catch fleeting glimpses of her worried smile across a wall of curious eyes. Then, they fight their way outside into the blinding morning light, he walks her to her college, stopping to buy a packet of cigarettes, the harsh unfiltered smoke that fed his lust, give me the taste of toasted tobacco, the billboards proclaimed, she would watch the butterfly of perspiration across his broad back, a parched wind from the baked pavements would rise up, under her sari, encircle her thighs. He buys bottled cold drinks, pulling them out from under slabs of filthy ice, they walk, sipping quickly, at the gates of her college he takes the empty bottle from her, his fingertips brush her hands, clammy cold, from the ice. Inside, she dashes to the bathroom, daubs her burning temples with tepid water, walks unsteadily up the stairs to her first class, in the cruel sunlight, a vapor of words rise from the pages of her book, the lecturer's voice cuts like a tired whip through the moan of the ceiling fans, she has never felt the heat so intensely, during the afternoon break, she sits with Sharmila on the shaded stairs, her inflamed head against the wall, is this love then, the searing of your physical being, the inflammation of your consciousness, a deep dryness in your throat, and yet he is but a passing fancy, a lonely traveler who is resting awhile before he journeys on, I think he loves you, Sharmila tells her, gravely, a little wistful, perhaps he will want to marry you. She turns her burning face to the wall and laughs, are you mad, he must have many girlfriends back at home, maybe he's married, even. But, as the sun dips in the sky, the fresh breath of afternoon sinks slowly into the classroom, she begins to wonder if he will be there after classes, they pause at the end of a poem, we have a few minutes to the end of the lesson, the Bengali professor pushes back her spectacles, Monideepa, will you give us a Tagore song? She clears her throat, fixes her eyes upon the chipped green paint of the desk,

Your eyes have pleaded with me for a song
Among flowers and stars, day and night, in the dusty light of dusk
You wonder why I do not sing
I lose my lyrics in my pain, I forget my tune

Tears well up in her eyes, she has always wished to be able to address someone with her song, she had thought, always, that it might be some young artist, the sweet torment of a burgeoning eternal love, she had hoped it would be one who would grasp the beauty of the poet's words, not a stranger who has no knowledge of her tongue, who gropes among the unknown words, the unfamiliar halftones, for an answer to his mute caress, she sings the same song, later that night, during a power cut, she can feel them absorbing the strains of its passion, the dark forms around her, her brother, Amrita, Gayatri, Manash, Tapan, they sit, crippled by sorrow, insensate with beauty, yet he is a distant shadow, struggling to comprehend the mood of her song, distracted by the faint smell of disinfectant that drifts in from the bathroom door by which he sits,

You have called to me in the fierce storm wind
from upon wild waters
in the thunder of mute clouds
in monsoon torrents, you have called me towards death
You wonder why I do not come
I cannot find my way to you across the seas.

A lizard hurries past his ear, does he dare ask for a translation? A strange silence sits upon the group, they are mute with emotion, and yet he asks if one of them might explain what the beautiful sounds mean. But as Amrita begins to translate, in her even, thoughtful voice, the lights come back on, and the television is turned on for the BBC serialization of Jane Austen's

Emma, they are transported suddenly to eighteenth-century England, he watches her, as she grapples with his history, the black-and-white shadows upon the screen are his world, somewhere across the oceans, perhaps some sharp-faced white woman waits for him to return. He rises to help the mother of one of the boys, whose house they are at, they have been invited for dinner, he cannot remember his name, Tapan, perhaps, he gets up to help her as she comes in with a pile of stainless-steel plates, they are all completely absorbed in *Emma*, one of them glances across, irritatedly, as the plates clash together like cymbals in his hands, but seeing him, breaks into an appreciative smile, he is a perfect gentleman, their English visitor.

He believes they have color television now, in Calcutta, that her parents have bought one with the money she sent them last year, they sent a photograph of her cousins and their children, seated around the television, it occupies the space where the lumbering old radio cabinet stood, as he remembers it, the crackle of cricket commentary on smoky winter afternoons, he waits for her to emerge from behind the faded curtains, secure that she is his, forever, that no man will lay his hands upon her except him, that there will be no lips upon hers but his, in the years to come, she will be there to gaze upon, to embrace in his impatient arms, the day of the wedding draws nearer, he watches with amusement, the growing panic, the elaborate plans, and during the cool nights, he dreams of making love to her, and he no longer has to choke back his imagination lest pleasure dissolve into unbearable pain, but in her eyes, from time to time, there is an excruciating sadness, a tinge of fear, a hint of doubt, that he tries to dispel with his smile, he takes her trembling hands into his, and tells her of his childhood, pale, eventless, until, one quiet afternoon, after a short, painful illness, his father died, papered walls that murmured of death, their grandmother gives them their tea in the cold clean kitchen, they are sent out into the bleak sunlight, he and his sister, he stood by her, as she stooped across the fence, and crushed nettles, one by one, with her bare fingers, if you crush them fast enough, they don't hurt, promise, she had always prided herself on the toughness of her skin, his sister, look, Tony, she would stick drawing pins into her arms, bet you can't, bet you'd bleed, whereas Heather would only turn somewhat green, she would amuse herself, on holiday afternoons, by pushing safety pins through a layer of her palm, she would wave her hands at him, a surreal landscape of aluminium, at nineteen, she had overdosed on Paracetamol, she never came out of her coma, that was his miserable past, she trembled with sadness when he spoke of his sister's hair, scattered like wheat across the hospital pillow, coiled among the tubes whose needles had burrowed through the resistant skin, he had watched death settle upon her, fresh as morning dew, and after they wheeled her away, he had walked with his mother into a shiftless summer morning, at home the results of her Advanced level exams have arrived in the early mail delivery, he creases the letter and shoves it under the mantel piece clock, and for months as telephone calls arrived for her, letters from her numerous penfriends all over the world, university mail, for many months, the bitter irony of death would be his only refuge from the vast emptiness she had left, yet this he could not explain to Moni, for she would shudder, a sudden incomprehension would drift upon the glaze of tears that has gathered upon her cloud-colored eyes, he cannot tell her that he has searched furiously among the morning mail for thick letters bearing her name, letters he will devour, and rip to shreds, he cannot tell her of his absurd satisfaction, as he pounds down upon the old typewriter, to whom it may concern, I regret to have to inform you of the sudden death of my sister, he runs his tongue across the envelope, and on sad silent evenings, he has looked into his mother's frozen eyes and cursed his sister, she has taken from them the semblance of peace that they had begun to cultivate, so many years after his father's death, she has left him without laughter, a hollow shell, and into his pillow, he weeps hot secret tears, for she has betrayed him, she, who with her eyes shining bright in the gas firelight, had kissed him goodnight, he had not known, as he passed her door, on his way to bed, that behind that glossy white, the Pierrot poster, she was washing down her tablets with harsh gin, all this he cannot tell her, and yet, in the stark stillness of a tropical winter afternoon, the image of Heather's death is imbued with such simple beauty that the bitter days that followed seem a vague shadow, an impalpable detail, he listens to his own words, clean and pure in the milky winter light, the convoluted poetry of her death that he has denied for so long.

And to her, on that motionless winter afternoon, when he had told her of his sister's death, the hollows deepening under his brow, to her, the horror of death had been enough to immerse her in deep sorrow, her eyes had brimmed with tears, today, as she leans back against the sharp counter, swilling bitter cold coffee against her palate, thoughts of death come blue as galactic shadow, death, perhaps, is the only ultimate resolution, perhaps if he finds them, mother and child, frozen, in a gas-filled bedroom, death might come, like delicious sleep, with the rich fragrance of rotting flowers, death may soothe her tired limbs, perhaps if he finds them, wrapped together, the liqueur of death upon their lips, perhaps then, even within her eternal slumber, she will sense his despair, or should she sit in the dark outside the child's room, to witness his anger and grief, the child in his arms, asleep forever, the smooth cheeks flushed with death, should she sit outside the door that she has closed to trap the sweet fumes of gas, the child will sink slowly into a deeper peace than that within which she dwells now, she will watch him shake the child's lifeless body, howl with grief, mad with hatred for her, she who had given her life, cushioned her in a warm sea of blood until she had pushed like mad horses into this world, he would seeth with revulsion, with disbelief, that she who had nourished her with her juices, cradled her within her fragile bones, that she might have wiped the stains of breath from the soft pouting lips, smoothed out the tiny lifeless fingers that had clutched at her in blind trust, the sounds of her merry laughter would be submerged within the voluptuous arms of death, the warmth of her soft skin would have folded into a deep core of peace, and in death she would have delivered her from the torment of life, the torture of desire, the pain of its fulfillment, the shards of its memory, the accursed duty of every creator, to quench the misery of passion in soft blood-smeared darkness, a silence as within a bell of cold metal, the delicate flames of life would have been trapped in a sea of glass, rather than, stoked by passion, burn her insides to ashes, so that she may never have to wake to a grim gray morning, and turn her last few hours of life about in her desiccated palms while death stands smiling at the foot of the bed, life would have become an old fickle friend, by then.

The child turns the pages of an old book of rhymes, who killed cock robin, I said the sparrow, with my bow and arrow, mother and daughter sit in Anna's bedroom, the autumn afternoon wavering outside, who killed cock robin? The child smooths out the page with her small plump hands, what does she know of death, they are sitting upon a faded rug in the small, warm room where, one rainy evening, many years ago, he had knelt above Anna's green eyes, insane with desire, he had plunged into the shadows of her flesh, and when he drew out and lay with his face upon her taut belly, the sweet sadness of guilt had quickened his passion, and he had dived deep within her again, the two of them are downstairs now, watching Tarkovsky's *Sacrifice* on videotape, the mournful sound of Swedish floats up and mingles with the whirr of the sewing machine, Anna's mother is taking in the party dress. Who killed cock robin, the startled bird lies with an arrow in its faded red chest, she brings her face to the book and inhales deeply of its ancient smell, the child imitates her, sniffing curiously at the stiff page, her mother has closed her eyes, she is back among the shelves of her college library, a drop of blood falls from her nose and blots upon the yellowed page, the girls help her to a chair, hold her head back, someone returns with a wet handkerchief, they fan her with limp exercise books, she has a strange sensation that she is dying for his love, a river of blood runs down the back of her throat, a comforting weakness seizes her limbs, this is love, a hot drop of blood on the oxidized pages of an old library book, it is there now, a tribute to their passion, young hands will grimace at the discoloration upon the page, they will muse, as she had done, of the fate of the many hands that have touched these desiccated leaves, freckled English girls in long frocks, smelling of lime juice and starch, the emancipated daughters of educated feudal lords, stiff in their homespun, a luxury of patriotism, rejecting the cheaper Manchester mill cloth so that they might choke the British economy, the pages had collected the tiny drops of sweat from many nervous fingers, perhaps a few anxious tears, and now the indelible stain of her blood lay smeared across its margins, coming home in the taxi, her head on Sharmila's lap, the euphoria of physical surrender leaves her suddenly, the blood has dried on the back of her throat and around her nostrils, a rancid sweat tickles her back, the piercing glare of the noon sun stabs through the cab window, the screech of bus horns knifes through a frolicsome nausea, she clutches at Sharmila's hand, at home, her mother runs a damp cloth over her body, she douses herself with talcum powder, slips into her nightgown, Sharmila smooths her hair back over the pillow, I can stay if you want, she says, I only have one class in the afternoon. No, you had better go, she whispers, her head throbs, what if he comes, you must explain to him, and all afternoon she is tortured by an unbearable conviction that upon hearing that she is not there, he may invite her alone, Sharmila, who has so much more to say to him than she, they may talk over coffee, wander through the Natural History Museum, she could take him to her Alipore home, an island of sterility, the spotless three-bedroomed flat, he could sit among the sea of cushions on their plush settee, and Sharmila's mother would entertain him in her convent-school English, immaculate servants would serve him coffee, so unlike their ragged maidservant, sullenly shaking sleep out of her tired eyes, Sharmila could take him to her bedroom to show him her paintings, no forbidding curtain divided the interior from the living room, only a sheet of chimes, that she would push aside to show him the way, and yet she knows, in the stale afternoon breeze, her nostrils caked with blood, she knows that he will merely be amused by her attention, that she too will seek to please him only for Moni's sake, it is her alone that he loves, more than he has ever loved anyone in the twenty-eight years of his life, more than he ever will love anyone, in the years to come.

The child turns the page, who caught his blood? I, said the Fish, with my little dish, I caught his blood, she laughs in limitless delight, the pouting fish balancing his dish of blood upon long fins, thin wisps of sunlight filter through the autumn clouds, she looks out upon the piles of dead leaves in the garden, this is how she has imagined the last day of life on earth to be, heaped autumn leaves that have not the energy to decompose, the clouds immobile in the sky, not the faintest breath of wind, pale sunlight falls upon the last man, clutching onto the last weak threads of his life, by the side of a stagnant pool, still as death, the ultimate quiet that would separate death from decay.

And time that she longs to hold back, barbed wire in her

palms, is sifting slowly through the crevices of her being, the afternoon has passed now, a torpid beast, crushing dead roots, leaving waterless windless plains in its wake, the premonition of this flat salt scent drove her, after lunch, to excuse herself, wander pretextless, down the streets, hang mute upon the steps of the crêperie, absorbed in the menu, crêpes carnival, stuffed with peppers and sea bass and cherry tomatoes, crêpes Normande, ham, honey and Camembert, crêpes Bretagne, myrtle-berries and monkfish, until a hand upon her shoulder heavy with nail varnish breaks her concentration, it is Lilian, long lost, she has not seen her since they left the cold flat in Turnpike Lane, Lilian, they worked together in the library, and afterwards, afraid to return to his futile eyes, she would linger, grateful confidante to Lilian's woes, and her pleasures, those that she would never comprehend, and yet felt that they might easily have been hers, of roasting the skin to fine raw honey, a new haircut that bared the back of her scalp, well almost, do you like it, Moni, do you think it looks good, at night she would loosen her dark waterfall of hair and wonder how it would feel to put a scissor to it, just under the soft earlobes, and how would it feel to thrash one's limbs all night to melancholy electric cacophony, while mother minded the child, I have to give her a meal of course, but it's still cheaper than a sitter, this curious love, she had come to accept, and one Friday when Lilian's mother was ill, she offered to look after the child, Anthony had been disturbed at her magnanimity, don't let her take advantage of you, he warned, you see, this flat simply isn't large enough, he had reasoned patiently, the girl arrived, thin, freckled, nervous, she had thought she might be younger, I've fed her, Lilian told her, taking in the dark looks that Anthony did not hesitate to send her way.

I've fed her, I hope she will be no trouble, so while they ate, the child sat, giggling nervously at some television program, but

then the TV had to be turned off, the table cleared for Anthony's
papers, the waves of sharp index cards, the child's face fell as
Anthony pushed in the switch, the picture blinked and was gone,
and within that instant, a fleeting pain crawled up within her
that he had enjoyed this little cruelty, but then he picked among
his books for one with pictures that she might like to see, and she
put an arm over the thin shoulders to steer her to the bedroom,
where she fell asleep, her cheek upon a glossy Man Ray photograph that had failed to interest her, and then when Anthony
had wanted to sleep, she had lifted her, light bird bones, laid her
down on the couch in the living room, she had meant to stay with
her, but he had insisted on making love, when she reemerged,
the girl was sitting up, wide-eyed, I was cold, she said. Lilian
came late, past two, on Monday morning there was a box of
chocolates, and she never left her with them again, how is your
daughter, she asked her, outside the crêperie, it's been so many
years, Lilian shrugged, you know what they're like at that age,
girls!

It had been many years, and that she should bump into her
seemed unbearably portentous, she had staggered then under
the weight of this ominous coincidence, but now, staring upon the
sea of dead leaves, the fine murmurs of autumn light within the
bonfire pile, it seems a gelid fixture in the ponderous firmament
of the afternoon, firm footsteps in the hallway, the dress has
been altered, Anna's mother eases it on the child, the girl
smooths the lace collar proudly over the blue velvet, you do have
some nice shoes for her, Moni? the old lady asks, glancing worriedly over her soiled pumps, and she remembers the chipped
white boots that Lilian's child wore, incongruous on her spindly
legs, their hard high tops had bruised her knees, and between
their gilt edges and the frayed hem of her green shorts, pale
thigh glistened like sweaty sandwich meat, and when she fell
asleep, her cheek upon the page, the tassels fluttering softly in

the summer breeze, she had struggled to unhinge them from her bare feet without waking her, and it had taken so long that when she had reached to move the head off the book, she had noticed to her horror that she had dribbled slightly upon the page, upon the violin-veiled waist, her saliva had trickled and thickened, and trembling, she had daubed it with tissue, closed the book hurriedly, ashamed of her fear, the girl rolled over upon her stomach, peeled spider limbs brushing against her, she had lain penitent fingers upon her barley hair, suddenly alive, and beautiful in the rays of the dying sun, how is your daughter, she had asked her, she must have grown since I saw her last.

You have not changed, Lilian told her, boring into her with emerald-shaded eyes, you have not changed at all, she stared at her helpless, she would not be able to tell her, but you have, you have changed, your skin falls in chicken folds from eyes of cracked glass, the proud hair, in spurious bleached ringlets, caresses vaguely the hard line of your shoulders, and your smile is weighed down by years of wasted desire, seven years ago, she had taken a photograph of her outside the public library, to take with her on her trip to Calcutta, and when Sharmila had demanded, almost reproachfully, tilting her maiden chin into the winter morning, to see what her new friends looked like, she had held out to her this testament, the fresh-faced young woman, sharp against the vast glass library doors, the white letters upon the door on either side of her seemed to emanate from her enormously oversized white pullover, like crisp antennae, Sharmila inspected the photograph closely, several times she feared she might make some comment whose beveled edges would rub painfully upon her, mirth that she could no longer share, and peering over her shoulder, she had thought wistfully how, some years ago, such a photograph would have provided endless hours of amusement, the lopsided pullover, hair, stiff as shards of black glass, eyes rimmed in luscious purple, a sudden sense of shame creeps upon her, but almost immediately a cold arrogance takes its place, she will laugh no longer, but it is she that has become privy to the secrets of another world, it is her horizons that have widened to embrace an alien meter of beauty, but Sharmila is silent, she rotates the photograph until the spiked hair hangs as it might have under gravity, and turning her hard eyes on Moni, she says, I read somewhere, recently, that you can read a person's character by turning them on their head, they both examine the rotated photograph, the face looks plumper somehow, bloated, placid, but Sharmila passes no judgment, a film of blood stretches taut between them, and have you no recent pictures of yourselves, Sharmila asks, she shakes her head, she has not brought any photographs of him, nothing to remind of the dark eyes, hovering upon the misery of impalpable deceit, Sharmila takes from her cloth bag an accordion album, there, she says, unpleating the sticky pages, I carry this everywhere, it is a blurred shot of them on the morning after the wedding, besprinkled with turmeric, the sunburned wrists send needles of violet into her skin, she begins to weep silently, the last glimpse of his bayoneted eyes, behind the airport glass, has left black chalk upon her tongue, which farewell is he mourning, that of her, or of his love for her, does the anguish in his eyes grow out of the humiliating struggle to banish the serpent haze of relief that engulfs him at the thought of her departure, he will pass the winter, biting cold typewriter steel, warring with the indignity of submitting to the burning fingers of lust that have begun to crawl under his shallow skin at the slightest wind from a woman's hair upon his cheek, the slightest bright dampness upon a lush lip, and though the hard plates of his skull had closed in to insulate his brain from the pounding of his pulse, the hammer blows barreled through bone like the tick of a pocket watch heard through wood. But he had not abandoned himself then to these thick murmurs, he had waited, until a year later, when he met

Anna, and the walls of his hollow castle had crumbled under a green wind, and the sky, which had been framed, for so long, by jagged walls, had reached to hold him in vast, pitiless embrace.

The jug of milk falls silently to the floor, Anna's fingers press on the pause button, she reverses the motion, why, why, he asks, they watch the shelf tremble, once again, the pitcher of milk flutters and falls, a glass womb releasing warm tears, she rewinds it again, this is my psychoanalysis, she explains, when I am able to watch the vessel drop without my blood rushing to the very top of my skull, I will know I am cured, she hits the buttons again, but it is like curing yourself of orgasm, he tells her, perhaps that is what I need, she replies enigmatically. Meanwhile, in the kitchen, the child is making a fuss over her tea, the egg is too runny, she begins to scream, Anna rushes to attend to her, and the milk jug hesitates, frozen on the edge of the shelf, and suddenly he is overcome by the sense that time is no gradual slope, but a sumptuous precipice, and he has yet to fall.

She watches Anna cutting soldiers out of cruel toast to coat in honeyed yolk, the floors gleam menacingly, and suddenly she remembers the sliced fruit laid bare to the roadside flies, unwashed thumbs pushing spiced potato mix into puffed wheat shells, to dip in tamarind juice diluted with drain water, rusty machines squeezing cane juice into grimy glasses, that was where she was taking her, what would she eat in that land of hunger, where children crammed their mouths with fetid soil to dull the burning of digestive juices against the thin bare walls of their gut, in the famine of '42 her father had seen a woman, insane with hunger, racing with her child to finish the bowl of food they shared, in those days they begged, not for rice, but for the thin scum of rice that papered against the boiling pot, and now, in the days of plenty, they thickened yogurt with lime, added ground glass to sugar, churned the seeds of spiteful yellow foxthorn flowers to adulterate mustard oil, and children lay blinded, crippled, unborn, would she boil the puny limbs of a feeble chicken for her every evening as she had seen her aunt do for her sons when they visited from Canada, bent cautiously over the kerosene stove, would she carry around heavy bottles of boiled water, delicately refuse store-bought sweets, she would never see such milk again as she was pushing away with her little hands now, she would have to drink the weak chalky suspension, diluted many times over, unless, perhaps, as she had imagined, last night, they might move into rural Bengal, there, the cowherd might milk the beast in front of her own eyes, as her aunt had done, many years ago, she had watched fascinated from the veranda of her village home, unbraiding her hair, as the maid drew up a pail of water from the well for her bath, the cow snorted, and left behind a dollop of dung, flies began to circle, how would she protect her precious cheeks, her plump arms, from the armies of insects that would thirst for her uninitiated blood, the hordes that would bore through the dusty bed nets to haunt her peaceful dreams, how would she shield her from the relentless sun, the sea of humanity that might engulf her in festival crowds, swarming streets, the gorged buses, her pale face squashed among perspiring bodies, her curls rent asunder by opposing currents of motion, until some friendly arms lifted her above, and battered and bruised she would be returned, to sweat forever in nightmares of suffocation, of heat and pain, of bodies bearing down upon her, of drowning in a sea of flesh.

The old lady lays a wrinkled, jeweled hand upon the child's head, a deep security floats upon the glow of the late afternoon, the smell of fresh rosemary, careful hands wipe egg stains off the child's chin, a hesitant shame stiffens within her as she imagines the old woman, driving through the London traffic in her silver Austin Mini, the birthday present, lovingly wrapped, on the seat beside her, a film of incomprehension will shroud those brittle blue eyes when she hears of her insolent game, a disbelief that will deepen into disgust, and yet, perhaps as she returns to the darkness of her enormous, empty home, she will count it as a battle won, for, often, when Moni has caught her breath at the pure happiness of their distant laughter, she has placed her calm fingers upon her elbow, distracted her with tales of days long gone, the crenellated edges of her elaborate past.

Time, he is telling Anna, has inspired a rich vertigo within me, I'm in no mood to continue watching the film, and brushing darkness from his eyes, he enters the kitchen, sits down at the pine table, he looks up at her, immobile among the verdant polyps that garnish the far corner, a spasm of sunshine flickers across her face, he is unexpectedly convulsed by the memory of a Cornish sunset whose burnished amber upon her skin he had tried to capture in the few frantic moments before the sea engulfed the gorged sun, but the shutter had jammed and the ardent light had remained a faint memory, a raw skein of copper, I did love her once, he muses, as seams of treacle close over the unsheathed nerve, he turns away and makes a face at the child, is met with a pout, milk-fringed, and as his thick eyebrows fall back into place, she notices suddenly how wide apart they are, his forehead rushes eagerly to meet his nose, a taut triangle in a sea of furrows, where a marksman might aim, if he were so inclined, it hangs like the blind white of fish eye that a lovesick warrior might have sought to pierce, under fathoms of golden water, in her land, before history, before time, and the capricious princess might rest her gaze upon his arms, scored deep from the tense string of his unyielding bow, and yet he will strive to see only the desperate dead white of the eye, marooned in silver scale, and if he is a good marksman he will see only the eye, untroubled, unrefracted under the suspension of bitter gold dust, and if he is a bad marksman, he will see a thousand eyes, in the mirror nest of fish scale, in the globules of gold, and, overwhelmed, he will pass his hands over his eyes, and return, without his princess, released from the curse of an archer that is never to see beyond his mark.

Merciless shadow drenches her, like the agony of song, long buried, breaking over her brow like a gray dream, her eyes are dead flowers held out, in desperation, to a storm. She will choke him with her sorrow, he thinks bitterly, after so many years, the trivial flames have risen, burning the sweet silence within her to thick ash, he will suffocate upon the embers of her charred song, the anguish of the poet gives shape to her own misery,

> the night wind has quenched my light
> and you come without haste to bid farewell
> passing upon this path in darkness
> the scent of night flower will drown you

but he will not drink of the frozen poison in her blood, crushed terra-cotta, and it is she who turns away from his caresses, she who presses cold slate upon his desire, memories of a turgid tropical dark stirring slowly within him, the formidable raw hunger that had doused his senses then comes back in fitful gusts to tease him, and then surrenders to the strains of riper desires, he turns his back upon the fallen ghosts of his lust, as he will turn his back upon her cancerous sorrow, so he resolves, he will not be smothered by the fat cinders of her forlorn dreams, he shuts his eyes to the dense vapors that rise through her tortured pores, and tries to imagine himself upon a sea cliff, the shriek of happy gulls, but he cannot shake himself so soon of the leaden shadows, and the feeling grows upon him that he is an intruder in this kitchen, for they both stand silent, the old woman's hands moving in careful circles through the fine hair upon his child's head, and she, distilling pain from the thickening shadows, the child slurps custard, let us play hide-and-seek, he suggests to her desperately.

The small mouth is wiped free of custard slime, the last

threads of yolk scraped off the soft chin, and then they creep through the darkened room, where Anna sits, taut, abandoned, and absorbed once more, the naked girl chasing birds down the hall, will she subject herself over and over again to this magical image also, to exorcise the darkness of her father's dreams, her father, the poet, who wrote of Anna in the fullness of womanhood that he knew he would never see. Anthony places a finger over his lips, sealed in desperate smile, the child falls silent, they creep away together on their hands and knees, into the hallway, still swaddled in amber light, he buries his eyes in his arm, I will count to ten, he tells her, and you must hide.

Purple hothouse flowers on slabs of black marble, leathery licorice drying in the desert sun, a ripe moon weeping milk, the marzipan dreams of her father had not been visionary, liver-rot had carved lush images of womanhood that Anna had defied, for after his death, the indeterminate color of her eyes had deepened to glass green, the skin shed the promise of color, and her hair acquired the texture of ice, and in her heart, a wheatfield grew where the poet had hoped blood roses would sprout under barbed wire, through the door Anthony can see a stiff shoulder, arched against the grainy television screen, he pauses, the child has hidden herself behind the old carved chest, one of her feet peeps out, muffled giggles, he must allow a few moments to pass before he pounces upon her, he must let her revel in the ingenuity of her choice, he must let her bask in her supposed concealment, but before her insulation becomes unbearable, he will pinch the fat toe, and pull her out, into his arms, it is your turn to count now, and no cheating, he walks deliberately towards the basement door, then creeps stealthily back towards the closet, parting stained sheepskin, he enters, closes the door gently behind.

It is the sister in Belgravia that fulfills the poet's prophecy, meant for this younger daughter, his favorite, it is the sister whose dark locks fall in lacquered delight over honey-roasted shoulders, but her insides are crammed with stiff tissue flowers, this the poet knew, and so he wrote only for the dreamy slip of a child that he had hoped to befriend in her prime, his younger daughter, but the image was corrupted by the decay of his flesh, and the ripening dark beauty of the older child, crinoline flowers line the contours of her heart, and Hungarian sheepdogs, legacy of a former marriage, wander her mirrored home like monstrous mops. He stifles sweet laughter, gurgling through, once more, out of damp stretches of mud, he buries his laughter in old alpaca, he has escaped the meshes of gloom that she had cast about him, thank heavens, but where is the darling child, he craves release from the musty prison of wool, he strains to hear the sounds of small feet, cracks open the closet door in an effort to reveal himself, but the hallway is silent, he sinks down against the back wall, this is an excellent opportunity for his life to veer into fantasy, if the wall should cave in, now, and he is plunged, not into Narnia, but into some chamber perhaps of a sleeping sprite, who will wake to the touch of his sandy lips, suck him into her wispy incorporeal being, and from then on, at every opportunity, he would creep stealthily into the closet, stumble through the wall into her amorphous arms, circles within circles of deceit, as a child he had pressed his hands to the back of his wardrobe, hoping desperately that the stark wood would yield, and eventually it had splintered, but when he looked through the crack and saw only the gloom of wallpaper, he had felt cheated, left behind.

He hears the wind, through muffled wool, as he has never heard it before, where is the child, and yet the cocoon of tweed and leather has an amniotic allure, he feels a deep peace gather within him, it is long since he has confined himself in so small a space, not since, perhaps, when in Amrita's grand mansion, he had stepped into a stately almirah, curious whether it would contain his length, and a great gust of monsoon wind had slammed shut the door, his first encounter with tropical dark, in the belly of an almirah, sandalwood-scented, his foot had fallen upon a prickly object, in the light, a dried orange, its ravaged flesh studded with cloves.

He will tell Anna of these ghostly minutes, tell her that perhaps for him, psychoanalysis should consist of a half hour in the closet, communing with wool and silk, closet therapy, a new nirvana, and in the land where he had gone to find peace, he had not lingered long enough in the spicy darkness of the old almirah to become familiar with its allure, instead he had stubbed his toe upon a hedgehog ball of cloves, and in his nervous ignorance he had taken it to be some talisman, and he had asked, at dinner, of its purpose, eager to comprehend all paraphernalia, all exotica (are we too cruel), eager to respect, he had asked its significance, and the mother-in-law had laughed a brittle laugh, and told him, it was a Victorian spiceball, in the thirties, perceiving his daughters to be complete in all but the fine art of Western homemaking, their father had engaged an English lady for this sole purpose, and she had tutored them in the creation of custards and casseroles, in the delicate art of laying a correct table, and escaping the tedium of hemming a large sheet by naming the four lengths by each continent, she had lectured them on the aspects of boiling mango pulp into jam, preserving soft guava in jelly, and she had imparted to them the fascinating exercise of spearing cloves into a juicy orange, to perfume the stagnant air within a damp wardrobe, and to embarrass young foreigners eager to find meaning in its voodoo texture, he laughs to himself, a cool spring torrent is rushing through the chinks in his consciousness, this is truly therapeutic, Trevor has been knitting recently, to free himself of tension, those terrible terrible knots, Anthony, in the hook of the shoulder blade, along my spine, the axis of my being, he did not knit creatively, just long scarves, spindly rivers of pied wool, and in the last few months, ever since he had applied for the position of director at the Institute, the scarves had been getting longer and longer, Jesus, where is the child, perhaps he has chosen too clever a hiding place, he should have just crouched under the stairs, or behind the door, he does not dare emerge for fear of seeing defeat in her eyes, his child, she must never know defeat, not yet, and never at his hands, his father, before he died, had played chess with him with terrifying concentration, and he had hated to feel himself a rival to the man he worshiped, his mind would cloud, the pieces run strange courses, and yet in victory his father would be disappointed by his son's lack of skill, have to be more alert, Tony, wake up, lad, can't muddle through life like a zombie, life, looming formidably outside the humpbacked window, life, lurking lampless in the dead fields across from school, life had played traitor to his father, and he had exchanged the prison of pain that life had become for the serene darkness of death.

And he had not done so badly in life, as his father might have thought, his troubled eyes behind the steam of his footbath, watching the pale boy playing with his tea, weak hands shaking upon the scones, distracted mouth, red-rimmed, will he ever find women, his father might have thought, his father, hammy progenitor, pub popular, he must have fretted over the future of his puny son, for it was only after his death that the son had begun to grow, grow furiously, his bones began to thicken, eyes settled deep into dark sockets, the cheeks caved, and furred, all too rapidly, there were children, he had heard, who went through phases of accelerated transformation with the plucking of their tonsils, and some who had stopped growing altogether, like the Indian child next door, not quite dwarf, and yet terribly stunted, her mother blamed her condition on her tonsils, and his mother had blamed the precocious growth of her son upon her husband's death, fatherless, her cherub had been compelled to sprout a horny patina, his hormones, in the hysteria of death, had run amok.

He even played rugby at school, of that his father would have been proud, he did not, however, enjoy cricket, his father's favorite game, and this had proved to be a major conversational drawback in India, where even the rarefied air of the theater group gatherings would burst into loud sparks over the controversial strategies of the current Test captain, and the pack of Australians they were playing were colored in demon flames, one fast bowler had a steel arm, he was told, while their best spinner was a polio cripple, the disease had configured his wrist in a fortuitous arc that sent googlies galloping down the wicket in trajectories as predictable as England's weather, enough to fox the most agile of batsmen, his googlies, they would lick their lips as if it were some delicacy, and he would see a googly, large lollipop-shaped cartwheeling at the feet of a perplexed cricket bat. One of them even wrote a short play, in which cricket became a metaphor for life, vicariously experienced, but he had floundered in the facile equation of the game's technicalities with the details of an old man's life—as he died, the patriarch conceded it had been an innings defeat, that sort of thing—it did not work, he knew the game too well to achieve artistic distance, a surgeon cannot think of the heart as an organ of love, or can he, he will never know, his knees are stiffening under heavy cashmere, where is the child, is she exploring, painstakingly, the multitude of rooms, will she open every other closet before she returns defeated to the hallway, perhaps like her, he should let a foot dangle out of the door, but wait, the door opens, but not with jerky child tugs but a clean strong sweep of adult force, he looks up into the bewildered eyes of his wife, and where there should have been laughter, a wall of sand rises, mightier than wool, he shakes himself free of the overcoats and steps out into the shadows, salt-smothered, once again, by her acid silence, etching deep into the moist darkness, she switches on a light, where is the child?

Through the door he can see Anna, stretched out upon the couch, asleep, lulled by the cicada static of the television, an ethereal evening slumber, curling towards him, he longs to sink into her hair, and in the room beyond, the kitchen, coldly lit, the shadow of her mother falls, the crisp pauses of a telephone conversation, in a dry whisper she explains, Helen is having one of her fits, fair Helen of Belgravia, prone to fitful depression, lovely Helen in her mansion of plaster, where dogs roam the iced hallways like misshapen mops, and you, my lovely, crushed glass in your eyes, what is this black fit that has fallen upon you, on this day of laughter and sunshine, the thin tar swirls about me, sucking me deep into the marshland that you have made of your existence, he begins to walk up the broad stairway, the child must still be upstairs, she follows him, world-weary, and strangely anxious, as if some harm might have come to her, and suddenly a chalk fear smothers his senses, he sees the child buried under a heap of memorabilia, crammed hastily into a closet, that she has opened in her search for him, the heavy debris of their past comes crashing down upon her light bones, he begins to run, turning on the lights one by one in the unused rooms, and in each room, the sterile order stares mercifully in contradiction to the all-too-vivid image of her bloody forehead under heavy picture frames, broken glass, an ancient gramophone, perhaps, he had seen one, somewhere here, yes, on that very day, that they had come here in the rain, insane with desire, searching for towels, they had opened many closets, and in one he had found the cobwebbed remains of an old gramophone, rich tears had gathered within him, and pressing Anna against the wall he had ruthlessly kissed her wet skin, this wall, and this room too is untouched, penitent, all the rooms are lit now, for the first time in a long time, the upstairs bulges with light, and no disaster seems to have befallen the child, but where is she, curled asleep perhaps under one of the beds, he turns into Anna's bedroom to make a more thorough search, he is upon his knees again, as he was, on that stormy afternoon, between the tremulous arc of her legs, he is upon his knees again on the cold wood, and the child is not under the bed, his hands stray across a dusty framed photograph of Anna with her father, already an old man, for he had married very late, the poet, the first fifty years of his life he had been absorbed in the import of silk from the Far East, and even, later, when he had given it all up for finer pursuits, poetry had never been a passion, Anna would say wistfully, never a torment, she had never seen him groan in the agony of fettered thought, and perhaps she had inherited from him an unimpassioned ease of creation, enemy of art, but no, no, he would kiss her sad lids, no, no, no, he knew she was capable of the most intense passion, he had tasted of it, yes, he found traces of it now, upon her soft lids, and yet he knew, as he consoled her, that she would never be overcome by the angst of an abandoned gramophone, such was the texture of her desire, that she would never be driven to wild despair by the memory of a windmill, as he had been, in sudden gusts, as a boy.

She lifts an edge of the patchwork coverlet, but the box springs are solid, the child cannot have squeezed under the squat legs, she stands up, her head reels, she must be somewhere, the girl, on the wall a photograph of Anna's father angled mercilessly, in her home there would be a garland of dry flowers about the frame, her grandmother had daubed her grandfather's portrait with sandalwood, hung flowers over the wooden frame, scaring geckos who made their home in its shelter, they would pop out and scurry back in again, as a child, she had hoped, although with disgust, that one might fall upon her head, for it was said that if a gecko should tumble down upon your head, you were sure to marry a king, and she had so wanted to marry a king, who would lift her upon his Pegasus, his birdking horse, and take her away into the clouds, the child cannot be upstairs, she thinks suddenly, looking desperately around again, this gentle room, bathed in soft lamplight, and this afternoon, Lilian had pleaded with her to accompany her on her weekly visit to her mother, the very same, whom she had lured with the promise of a meal, sticky sausage and mash, plastic-wrapped steak and kidney perhaps, to mind the spindly girl in tasseled vinyl boots and green shorts, she was feeble now, wheelchair-bound, but lived on her own still, the tiny council flat, claustrophobic orange whorls upon the carpet, Lilian set down the groceries in the inlet of light that was the kitchen, remember Moni, mum, we worked together at the library, she minded Clare once, when you had the flu, Clare, of course, that was the child's name, thin, pale fingers, translucent almost, abandoned upon the glossy page, the Man Ray photograph that she had dribbled upon, and the hair, strangely alive, crawling with light, a sad summer sunset, a field of dead salt.

The child cannot be upstairs, she rushes down, perhaps she has wandered into the garden, in the dark, fallen into the pond, her heart begins to pound, and if the child were to be found now, drowned among the pale goldfish, the spidery plants, floating like a dead petal upon the dark waters, would it be madness that would descend upon her, soothing endless night, or would she embrace it as an eventuality of her fate, her destiny, that had revealed itself to her, this morning, when thoughts of smothering the life that had grown within her came crashing in great bitter waves, and the realization comes to her, as she frantically tries the glass door to the garden, that even if it is madness that awaits, she will pause first to relish his agony, that by hiding in a closet, and crouching callously for so long within the secure darkness, he has sent her to her death.

But the French doors are locked tight, outside the night hangs deep, bright ink, the color of the calligraphy with which she liked to fill her diaries as a young girl, oh she hated blue ink, the color of dull shadow, I cannot abide your bourgeois caprices, her brother had told her, she turns away from the steady darkness, and notices that the basement door is ajar, she stops to listen, curious popping sounds are coming from somewhere, surely the child has not been swallowed by the washing machine, like some anti-mechanization film of the the sixties, she pushes open the door, the sounds do, indeed, issue from the bowels of the house, she climbs cautiously down the steep stairs, and there she is, in a sea of styrofoam beads, popping them one by one with absolute absorption, a large computer box lies on its side, the old lady's latest toy, you don't know how useful it is for keeping accounts and things, dear, I've even started writing my letters on it, the child looks up, flushed with guilt, come on, she says, pulling her up, we will put all of that back in the box, and then we're going home.

Upstairs, he is still groveling upon floors, under beds, behind wardrobes, hands cobwebbed, nails green with dust, I have found her, she tells him, she was in the basement, he would have loved to hear that she was popping styrofoam beads for half an hour, but she will deny him this source of mirth.

They say their goodbyes, is this the last she will see of the old lady, crinkled cheek brushing against hers, perhaps a long letter will arrive, word-processed, pleading her to return, or perhaps there will be silence, the raw silence of an unresolved relationship, her eyes cloud with tears, she does not want to hurt her, the last brave wave of the stiff fingers, before she is engulfed once again by her cavernous home, will she wander now, switching off the lights that they have left on, the upstairs, brimming with light, one by one, the windows will darken again.

And among the dusky streets of London, she feels reproach, she had wanted to make this her home, and instead the city had remained stately and aloof, the dispassionate streets look upon her now, silent, ignoring the secret they share, and yet, ten years ago, every alleyway in Ballygunge had trembled with the heaviness of her departure, weeping puddles upon the cracked pavements, they had turned away, indignant, betrayed, she will go back to them, the narrow pitted streets, cloaked in a miasma of car fumes, the dung smoke of a thousand clay ovens. In the car mirror, their eyes are locked in some silent game, Anna sits behind her, and he is in the driver's seat, the lights turn, his eyes move to the road. She reflects sadly that the day has almost passed, and she has not relished the irony of each moment, each slow step towards doom, she has not smiled, cruel and confident, over their childish anticipation, their futile pleasure, a strong perfume of disaster does not hang heavy in the air, instead, the day has passed, save for the cruel pinprick of panic over the child's disappearance, it has passed listless, dull.

After dinner, an oppressive melancholy invades them as they watch the news, he gets up, unable to bear it any longer, throws on his coat, I'm going for a walk, he tells them, the door bangs shut, he cannot understand why the bubble has burst, why, instead of the long, slow smiles, the tender sorrow of her dignified silence, there is an abrasive misery in her eyes, why, on this day, of all days, she is mute with a sour despair, an unfamiliar gloom gathers within him, perhaps they cannot go on like this, after all, perhaps he should leave her, visit the child on weekends, they can live with his mother in Bristol, what excuse can he give her, does he need to give her an excuse, she is a lump of clay in his hands, besides, he thinks bitterly, what choice does she have, where can she go within this wide world without his support, he has sheltered her within his palms as the bud he had plucked, untimely, intoxicated by its incomplete scent, he had treasured in his glass house until he found that she would not

bloom in her new surrounds, and if she had suffered for that, he
had suffered more, as he had come to terms with the bitter truth
that the unadulterated passion he had felt for her under tropical
skies was not to last forever, that a deep intellectual void was
eating away at his wonder, his enchantment, he could not tell
her of what he wrote on the typewriter, into the early hours of
the morning, his frustration remained dammed within him, and
it was more painful than the concealment of his sharp desire in
the thin tropical darkness, and he had smiled ironically as she
helped him pack his index cards, the night before they moved to
their new home, months after he had surrendered his dream of
a lectureship in drama for a well-paid administrative job that
had come his way, she sorted carefully through his stacks of
index cards, put them neatly into a cardboard box, and they
were there still, in the room where she ironed his shirts, the
tedious length of her saris, it was to have been a study of sorts,
they lay in the corner, his boxes of papers, the thick journals he
had kept in India, notes on Bengali theater that he interspersed
with declarations of his love, he had mused in the early days of
their love that he might dedicate his thesis to her, his tropical
dream, she dwells with Beauty—Beauty that must die, perplex
his examiners with their warm secret, and perhaps, bold in his
distance, he would send her a copy by sea mail, she would
fumble with the salt-stained wrappings, her eyes would tremble
as they fell upon the page, To M., she dwells Beauty—Beauty
that must die, words whispered in the dense calm of rain, a
damp ache in his throat, the cold of the cement floor eating
through into his thighs as he lay and drank deeply of her eyes,
the soft sea of cloth upon her bosom, she would remember the
sharp gasps of desire that escaped his blistered lips as she
stooped to gather the cards, as she brushed by him to rouse the
maid, she would hold the heavy tome to her breast and weep,
she would treasure it among her volumes of poetry until, riddled

by silverfish, it would crumble into tropical dust, instead she had shed bitter tears over the typewriter that lay unused in the corner, the sheaves of papers gathering dust, the unpacked boxes, as evening upon evening passed with the glitter of lamplight upon the wet leaves. He shook off the grime of a dull day's work, and if he knelt down among the boxes, his mind would fill, once again, with the skeleton of the crane that hung outside his office window, whose angular impatience he would observe as he dictated letters. He would push aside the dusty cartons, tomorrow, perhaps, he would tell her apologetically, and in the living room, he would drown the murmurs of her song with his television remote control. It was Anna who had led him back into the world to which he belonged, taught him to breathe richly, again, of life. Their first stolen weekend alone, in a cottage in the Cotswolds, they had been forced to drink calvados to keep warm, while he sucked cold ink off his fingers, Anna had leaned over his shoulder, her hair, a sea of pale gold, lapping against the pages of his first play, he had seized her frozen fingers and kissed them with wild hope, and even though the stiff pages of his passionate endeavor still lay locked in Anna's desk drawer along with her black-and-white photographs of his windswept face, he had found his way, through her, into the circles to which he had always aspired, ever since he came to London, at eighteen, to study English literature at University College, that first lonely evening, staring into the faded linoleum floor, he had longed for success, more than the love of a woman, and now, that it had come within his reach, now, of all times, that *she* should quell the festive turbulence of his blood with her troubled eyes, he kneels down in a pile of wet leaves, in the thin darkness, and begs for deliverance from her mournful gaze. Many years ago, he had stood back, horrified, and watched his passion for her melt like candlewax, and he had rejoiced when a deep affection had come to take its place, he had held her small warm hands against his face with new joy, pressed his lips to the flesh that he no longer desired, placed his hand over the soft cage of bones that sheltered his child, he watched her tenderly as she drifted into a gentle sleep beside him upon the ferry, cradled her head on his chest, if they were to live on the memory of their love alone, that would be enough, for he had felt no greater sadness than to see their love pass, like wind through his fingers, he felt himself wiped clean of that rich emotion that had driven him through the wild heat to wait foolishly outside the stern gates of her college praying that she would emerge, he would gaze, disbelieving, at the unruffled fingers that had pro-pelled him to such ecstasy by their mere touch upon his palm, he had bathed her swollen ankles with tears, on the first night that he returned with the smell of another woman deep within him, while she slept, he had wept at the foot of their bed, his knees bruised from the hard wooden floor of Anna's childhood room, he had crept in beside her, and spilled heavy, sweet tears upon the field of hair that stretched across his pillow, in the darkness he had listened for the heartbeats of their child while the linger-ing scent of Anna's ivory flesh preyed upon sleep, and in his pain, he had reasoned that even if he had left her behind to the smoky Calcutta winters, he would have felt, even more sharply, that he was betraying their love, for he would not have tired of the memory of her eyes as quickly as he had become immune to their mystifying presence, he kneels among a pile of dead leaves, and for the first time in years, he mourns the death of their passion, the brittle shell of their tropical lust.

A fine rain begins to fall, the agony of inadequate raindrops upon his ravaged face, he pushes back his damp hair, when he returns he will tell her that she must recover, for the child's sake, she must cast off her gloom, he finds her, in their bedroom, sitting among a pile of her best saris, is she musing over which to wear? No, she tells him, Anna has decided to wear a sari to the party, she had picked out among her most expensive garments the heavy red benarasi that she had worn at their wedding, whose curious folds he had moved aside in deep intoxication, so that he might cup the smoothness of her thighs, she had tried to teach Anna how to wear it, her hand firm upon her warm, taut belly, she had tucked in the stiff folds, and so she would appear perhaps, on Monday afternoon, to his muddy eyes, an incongruous phantom, a mockery of the past that he had destroyed, and now she surveys the rest of her wardrobe and wonders calmly what she might take back with her, her departure now seems matter of course, there is no mystery, no secret joy, she sits among her stiff clothes and glances across at his damp, unshaven face, she feels they are packing for a trip, many years ago, she had sat upon this bed and sifted through her clothes, wondering what she might take to the lavender hills of Provence where they had rented a cottage with Trevor and his new girlfriend Anna, whom she had met only once, at a confusing party in Lewisham, she had stood stiffly at his side, while he introduced her, he had known her father well, he said, and known her since she was a slip of a girl, and she had looked upon her bored green eyes, the pale hair drawn back into a glistening French braid, and she had thought that she might have been beautiful if her nose were a little sharper, her mouth not quite so wide, although her presence inspired a certain awe, she was the daughter of a poet, Anthony had told her as they drove home through the East End, an insignificant poet, a gentleman who had dabbled in the arts as a pastime rather than a passion, her attention had been diverted by the sad shadows of the garroted alleyways that she would come to know so well, years later, in her job as a translator of medical complaints, she would become familiar with the dense smell of spice trapped in winter wool, of old oil and fungus, poverty and filth took on a different shape in these temperate climes, she remembered the stench of boiled cabbage soup and perspiration in the Himalayan slums, a holi-day in Darjeeling, the undisguised distillates of humanity that burnt off in thin wisps from the baked Calcutta pavements, condensed in the cold damp of the hills, an old fermentation rose from the thin wooden slats of the dense settlements, she held her nose as she cradled a rosy-cheeked Tibetan child on her lap in the crowded train that wound its way slothfully up the sodden hillside, a clot of green snot blocked a squat nostril, she turned away nauseated, her brother remarked grimly that if she was to be truly human she must overcome her squeamishness, she must subordinate her disgust for the unclean to her desire to love mankind, and she had clutched the girl to her breast, in wild defiance of her nausea, eyeing fearfully the hard lice eggs that clustered in her cold, silken hair. As the train looped slowly up into the mountains, she breathed deeply of the damp fragrance of wet ferns against the rock walls, tall Japanese cedars dripped their sweet juices upon the moss, and yet the rancid layers of the child's rags bit deeply into her senses, she refused food, her mother shrugged and doled out puffed bread and potato curry to her brother and her father, she watched her family eat, their gaze fastened upon their food to avoid the million hungry eyes, mothers turned their children's faces to the bright hillside mists rubbing at the train windows, and so it had been and would ever be, on every journey, except those they took in the insulated comfort of air-conditioned sleepers, famished eyes would fall upon them, the food would turn to cinder in her mouth, she would shrink from the diseased hands that stretched in through the train window, an impatient tea vendor would push the beg-gar rudely aside, raw earthenware cups, damp with tea, rough against her lips, as the train moved out of the station, she would watch the hungry eyes pass, empty cups would be flung out of the window, crash against the rail tracks, ashes to ashes, dust to dust.

She moves her hands across the smooth surfaces of silk, the heavy embroidery, her wedding trousseau, he sits hunched upon the low dresser, in his eyes the same frightened despair as when he watched her, many years ago, put together her clothes for their holiday, when they drove into the belly of the ferry, Trevor and Anna frolicking in the back seat, the reek of the rotting sea had promised disaster, he clenched his lips, his knuckles stood out deathly white as he gripped the wheel, as they were disgorged upon French soil, she fell into an impenetrable slumber, the first languor of an unsuspected pregnancy stirring in her veins, and hours later, he had given the wheel to Trevor, climbed into the backseat, and between fits of exhausted sleep, he had contemplated the strange beauty of the girl beside him, daughter of the poet, whose works he had perused recently out of curiosity for those wonderful eyes, and so we live on through our children, he thought, obscure volumes are pulled out from thick dust by one enchanted by the sea green of eyes that have come forth from the author's loins, trembling hands search the forgotten pages for words and images, a mist of gold that is a child's hair, small palms cradling warm bird's eggs,

Whispers and small laughter between leaves and hurrying feet
Under sleep, where all the waters meet.

Bowsprit cracked with ice and paint cracked with heat.
I made this, I have forgotten
And remember.

When his own daughter was born, some months later, he had searched among the corpus of English poetry to give expression to the well of emotion within himself, *I tremble, as one who must view, In the crystal a doom he could never deflect—yes, I too, Am fruitlessly shaken*, he had wept, his face upon the cold sill, in the fear that he would never be able to protect her from pain. No, he could not survive without the steady sound of her shallow breath behind the white door, he would not be able to bear to see her only on weekends, watch her grow into a stranger, as doubtless she would, even under the same roof, someday she would despise him for what he had done to her mother, as his sister had hated the dead man who tortured their mother and then in death, deserted her, yet, when he felt her sweet breath upon his cheek, as he knelt down close beside her, she drew for him a rabbit with her stubby crayons, he would feel then, as he gazed in wonder upon the pale brow, wrinkled in concentration, he would feel then, that nothing mattered more,

> What seas what shores what granite islands towards my timbers
> And woodthrush calling through the fog
> My daughter.

The soft hills of Burgundy rushed by, feigning sleep, he let his head fall close to hers, and to his delighted surprise she laid a soft hand upon his delirious brow, smoothed aside the locks of dark hair that hid his half-closed eyes, he smiled and sank down upon her shoulder, burrowing deep into the almond scent of her neck, feigning sleep; he caught in his lips some slippery strands of hair, Trevor drew up into a lay-by, he pretended to wake from some sweet dream, they stretched and drank to a pale French dawn and he kissed with renewed tenderness the heavy lids of his wife, shivering in the early-morning cold, and then as she slept upon his lap and Trevor snored in the front seat, while Anna drove, they had talked of her father's poetry, his mind taut with the lack of sleep, and so the flame within him had burned thicker, until, one sad night, in the olive darkness, as they walked alone among the short shadows of the trees, he had seized her proud shoulders and sought the wounded curve of her lips, in the curdled darkness, he had crushed the last fragments of his absurd fidelity upon her warm flesh, and even as he drew back, a strange suspicion had taken hold of him, that he had stifled their budding emotions with that desperate kiss, he had sucked out from within her, with his hasty lips, the violent passion that had condensed between them, and as he fought against the voluptuous darkness to hold together the fickle fragments of his new passion, her song had drifted towards them across the moonlit pebbles, I will not go into the drunken spring winds, he had stood in the shadow of her dark eyes, convulsed with desire, that night he had made furious love to her, from between his frantic fingers she had watched the trembling moon, the pitted orb that a young revolutionary, her brother's favorite poet, had likened to charred bread in the eyes of the hungry.

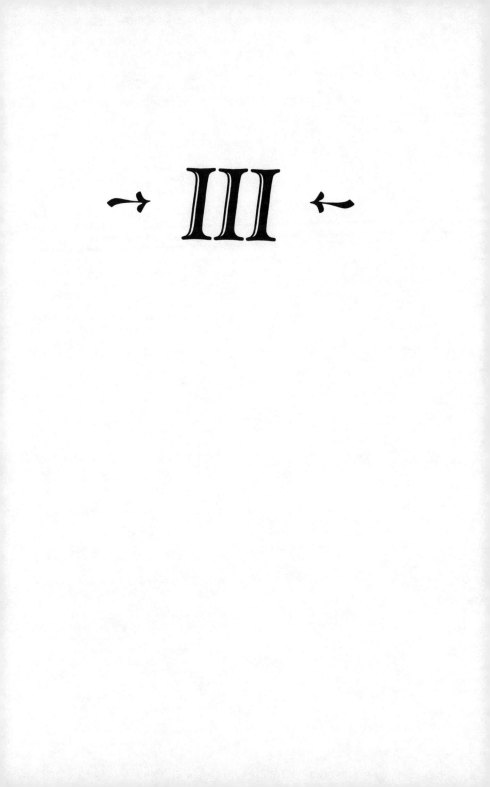

She wakes from a dream of death and wet marigolds, and for the first time in many years, the sheets beside her are cold with his absence, the smell of burnt bread wafts from under the closed door, the sweet peace of her dream fades suddenly within her, she will miss his warmth, the comforting tension of the shared sheet as he stirs in his sleep, the steam of his breath upon her anguished eyes, she will miss his tall shadow behind the door, he pushes in with a tray of tea and blackened toast, he sits upon the bed beside her and pours the tea, she will miss the pressure of his limbs outside the bedclothes, she will miss the shadow of porcelain upon his pale palms, the dark stain of tea upon his lips, he sets down his teacup and leans down upon her, burying his face on her breast, she will miss the dry darkness of his unruly hair against her skin, he turns his face so that his hot breath brushes against her arm, our daughter will be six years old tomorrow, he says.

A faint crack of thunder brings with it the thrill of doom, all this she has loved, all this she will leave, he mistakes the sudden flicker of excitement in her eyes for that of a renewed interest in the party, he covers her face with glad kisses,

> on this last night of spring, I have come empty-handed, garland-
> less
> a silent flute cries, the smile dies on your lips
> in your eyes a wet indignation
> when did this spring pass by, where is my song?

She holds a favorite blue bowl over the bathtub, deciding whether to let it crash against the stark porcelain, many years ago, she had been seized by a craving for a particular shade of blue, they had hunted high and low for the blue that she sought, many years ago, he had watched with amused delight as she turned each object in her hand, a glass vase, a china jar, and shook her head in disappointment, they had scoured the city for the blue that she desired, and finally, she had found it, the blue of a spent flame, captured in the glaze of a piece of cheap pottery, for many years the bowl had held a bandaged ostrich egg, until someone had remarked that because it had the shape of an oversize eggcup, the ensemble looked like some hideous work of conceptual art, like a plaster of Paris pizza, and the egg had been allowed to come into its own upon a wooden shelf until the neighbor's cat smashed it to bits during a toothpaste commercial, and she had rescued the bowl, filled it with dried lavender and placed it in the bathroom, so that she might reach out as she relaxed in her bath and run her steaming fingers upon its flickering blue, and she lets it drop, it breaks neatly in two, the dusty lavender sticks to the moist walls of the tub, Anthony bangs at the bathroom door, what happened, he asks, what have you done, he picks up the fragments of the bowl, perhaps we should never have separated it from the ostrich egg, he says. When she was a child, if she wanted something very badly, she would make her own secret sacrifice to God, some irrevocable deed, shearing the silver hair of her favorite doll, the broken blue bowl is her first concrete recognition of approaching disaster, her first rebellion, and yet as she studies her neglected body in the bathroom mirror, she wonders if there would not be more dignity in telling him, now, or no, perhaps tomorrow, after the party, that she is leaving him forever, her mind chills as she envisages the broad smile upon his face, she will leave him, will she, but it could not even go that far, the dry words would stick in her throat, her command of the language would fail her, how did one say, without melodrama, in this language that she had worshiped as a girl, how did one measure out one's words, how could she say, without humiliating herself, that she must leave him, that she would take the child with her, he would do all that was within his means to prevent her, she has no alternative but to steal away, without rebellion, it is not in her power to offer an explanation, she must shatter glass behind closed doors, and many years ago, she had turned her face away from the frustrated eyes of a young American who had pleaded with her to follow him across the Atlantic, it would have been simple then, to have gathered the child in her arms and walked out with him, but she had turned away, the numbness within her churned to fear, who knows what new pain might have awaited her in that vast land, many years ago, he had arrived at their door, shaking with fever, he had just spent six months in India, in Calcutta he had met Moni's brother, who had given him their address. He lay for days in a stupor, she had rinsed his forehead with damp cloths, fed him chicken stew, she had inhaled the thick aroma of a tropical fever, she felt the heat of his diseased blood coursing madly through his temples, as the child played at her feet she would listen for his sounds in the small room upstairs, and when he was well enough, he would come down and sit with her, swathed in blankets, he would suddenly doze off, his mouth gaping against the plaid, come away with me, he had said, one evening, why are you staying with him, you are wasted here, come away with me, believe me, you would love New York, and where my parents live, in Vermont, at this time of the year, the hills are flaming with the colors of fall, your English autumn is like death, the leaves do not wait to ripen upon the branches, they drop off dead, like thin cardboard, come away from this morbid island, and infuriated by her hollow smile, he had packed his duffel bags and left without a word, she had heard him go, horribly awake in the gray dawn, while Anthony muttered in his sleep, she had heard the sounds of his heavy footsteps dragging his bags down the stairs, the front door closed gently shut, she lay, frozen, indignant that his affections could have so quickly turned to exasperation, and yet she had felt nothing for him, no whisper of passion for the sculpted brow she had wiped with camphor, the thin nostrils, quivering with fever, death steam upon his lips, now, as she remembers his flushed, young face, she is stirred by a mild longing to have tasted the warmth of his arrogant lips, but all that had appealed to her then was the long stretches of profound silence between them, while she stared into the flames, he had gazed up at the ceiling, leaning back on his large, thin hands, she had never known anyone to be so comfortable with silence.

Silence, her mute companion of lonely evenings, a discerning audience of her song, silence had been an elusive spirit in her metropolitan childhood, had befriended her in North London, here she had found a deeper silence than even the quiet before a tropical storm, the still rushes, the frightened birds, once, she had lingered, in a field of mustard, in the windless core of a storm, in such an hour, a dark village maiden had lifted her ebony eyes to the poet,

> like black clouds gathering at the corners of a May sky
> like soft black shadows descending upon June forests,
> in this way the mirth of a July evening fades suddenly away.

The rain whipped around her as she fought her way back to her aunt's house, inside, rivulets of rainwater forced their way through closed shutters, trickled through the whitewash to collect in chalky puddles on the floor. She watched the heavy hips of her aunt as she bent down to mop up the rainwater and she wondered how it was to know that these bones would never hold the growing warmth of a child, on her wedding day she had watched her kneel upon the chipped red cement floor of the rented house and decorate it with a milky solution of ground rice that dried hard and white in large spirals of flowers and sea shells, she had watched the heavy hips shift as she moved round the circle, her fingers configured into a stylus for the murky fluid in her palm, she had looked upon her and wondered that one sad morning many years ago, it was she that had watched the preparations for her wedding, her young limbs smeared with turmeric, and her tender hopes had been shattered by the cold eyes that pierced her veil, the stranger that was to be her husband. And, shivering with sweet sad sorrow on that fateful winter morning, Moni had wondered, as she studied the wooden grace of her aunt's arm sweeping in complicated arcs across the red floor, what she had gained by leaving a home, an indifferent husband, a cruel mother-in-law, to live alone, among the blunt banyans, to sit in her bamboo rocking chair on her veranda and read endless novels, did she not, on some still summer evening, lift her eyes to a glorious sunset, and feel, like the poet:

If you did not give me love
Why paint the dawn sky with such song
Why thread garlands of stars
Why make a field of flowers my bed
Why does the south wind whisper secrets in my ear?
If you did not give poetry to my soul
Why does the sky stare like that upon my face
And why do sudden fits of madness grip my heart?
I set sail upon seas whose shores I know not.

Her aunt had died alone, last year, a malignancy that she had ignored had eaten through her disused flesh, her brother told her, on the shadowy afternoon that he arrived, they sat in the front room, and he told her, that she had died alone, in the dense dark of a village night, the maid had found her senseless, and she had died in the country hospital before his train had pulled into the desolate station, later that day many of her old students had appeared, helped him carry her to the burning ghats, he had bitten back his disgust, his deep bitterness, at their vehement religious chants, Hari bole, give me another, Hari bole, louder now, Hari bole, softer now, Hari bole, everybody then, Hari bole, he had come back to Calcutta with her warm ashes, Moni had wept long upon the gray carpet, and yet, she remembered, death had always lurked in the slow circles of her calcified breasts, flesh that might have remained pliant under a man's touch had hardened and decayed, so she had felt, every time her aunt held her in glad embrace, her dry lips upon her forehead, in her breath, there was the desiccation of death, not the moist, voluptuous death that she had dreamt of last night, but a death like hot salt, burning upon the tongue. Perhaps as the years go by, death will appear to her, not stained with crushed flowers, but as dry bone dust upon taut blades of grass, as she learns to live without his gentle hands upon her, without the warm hollows of his sleep-soothed eyes. She will twist tropical creepers between her fingers and her parched skin will drink gladly of their bruised juices.

She will steal away like a sorry child, without dignity, she cannot confront him, the language of their love was silence, but now the space between them is dull with forgotten emotion, she cannot use silence to convey her pain, they stand upon Parliament Hill, the child unraveling her kite, Anna's hair shimmers like a net upon the morning wind, the smoky profile of the city stretches out in the distance, she is still a stranger to this land, she watches the dark lust upon his eyes as they twist about in the sea of pale gold that blows upon his face, her hair, she reaches out for his trembling hand, he looks round in surprise, she has not reached for him in many years, she takes his quivering hand in hers, she will know the depth of his desire, she will feel the keenness of his lust, she will intercept the waves of passion that roll towards the emerald eyes, she must remember how much he once loved her to enjoy the prospect of leaving him, for she will not have the pleasure of his despair, she must steal away, when he would least suspect, in the few holy hours before a birthday party, he will return to an empty house, she must imagine his disbelief, his grief, she must carry with her the image of his hunched form at the foot of the stairs, among the monstrous stuffed animals, the muscles in his back stiff with sorrow. He turns away from Anna to smile at her, encircle her waist with his arm, and within her, there grows a shadow of the possessive peace that would descend upon her in the days when he would leave the hungry eyes of some woman at a party to push his way through the crowds towards her, smiling, smiling, through the crowd, he had loved her once, this she must remember if she is to exult in her departure. And yet as the memories crowd upon her, sudden and thick, she is seized by a new fear that in the silence of tropical afternoons, she will listen, shamefully, for his footfall, the bitter hope that he will come back for her may shroud her mind, she may listen, confused, for the sounds of his taxi drawing up outside, the jingle of insubstantial coins as he pays the driver, so that she may rush into her room, her heart pounding wildly to bury her face in a book of poetry as she had done, many years ago, she would sit at her desk and wait for the doorbell to ring, she would hear her brother stir in the living room, waking from his afternoon nap, later he would come in to brush his hair, the saheb's here, he would say, shaking the sleep out of his eyes, go and talk to him, he's obviously here to see you, go and talk to the poor sod, she would shrug her shoulders, I have to study, and she would listen to the vague noises of their conversation beyond the blue whitewash, the click of match flame as they lit their cigarettes, her brother smoked in front of their parents, another habit her uncles could not tolerate, and towards the evening, he would come in again, get dressed, he would command, we are going out for a meal, and she would sit silent with her food, warm with their talk around her, their incomprehensible references, their painstaking analyses of works of art that had left her only with the dense beauty of an unknown mood, she listened without comment, even when Anthony tried to draw her in, she might smile, shake her head, I do not know what the artist was trying to say, I do not know at all, it struck her now that he had thought her brother something of a fool, found his politics deplorably naive, last year, after watching *An Enemy of the People* at the Young Vic, Anna had taken them to the tapas bar on The Cut, and in between the loud bouts of the electric guitar, Anthony had dismissed her brother's opinions with a casual irritation that had pierced her heart, he had brushed aside his arguments with a tired smile, his eyes upon Anna, and her brother had not noticed the contorted desire within those dark eyes, floating ever upon the tall woman beside him, he had thought, instead, that she was his sister's friend, a loving friend who insisted upon feeding her the last baby squid, her brother had been hungry when they came back home, Anthony went straight to bed, he had asked, Moni, do you have anything in the fridge, I don't feel as if I've eaten, and while he wolfed down cold rice and some lentils she had warmed, she had suddenly gripped his arm, Mrs. Stockman, she said, now I remember where we have seen her before, dada, do you remember *Fawlty Towers*? Did he remember, those Tuesday evenings they would knock shyly upon their neighbor's door, they did not have a television then, could we watch *Fawlty Towers*, they would be let in, take their shoes off before entering the darkened room, where the fluorescent screen hummed, the household crowded upon the bed, a program on health would be ending, a strange thrill would run through her, the familiar tune, she would seat herself discreetly in the back, her shoulder against the ghostly bednet pole, a plate of sweets would be pushed her way, don't know how you understand what they say, the lady would murmur affectionately, a strong smell of betel juice came from the caverns of her mouth, blistered by her addiction to paan, the triangular pouch of betel leaf that held sweet spices, shut up, will you, her husband would bark, and she would slip away, her duty done, you mustn't give me sweets every time, Moni would tell her after the program while she put her shoes back on, else I shall have to stop coming, but her insides would turn cold at the thought, those Tuesday afternoons there would be a special pleasure in walking back from school, *Fawlty Towers.*

The kite soars into the air, she longs for the trees around her to burst into flame, into a crowd of bees that will descend upon her in deliberate fury and sting her senseless, images of his charred bones mingle with the smell of ripe jackfruit in her mind, she sees herself with the child, standing at their grave, a Victorian ending, the child clings to the black folds of her garments while they watch the wet earth scatter upon the single coffin that holds them, her husband and his lover, entwined in the sweet agony of death, instead, in the years to come, their lonely lives will diverge, and on a bleak autumn morning, he will take up his pen and write to his daughter, my darling, I remember a morning, so many years ago, we flew kites upon the heath, you laughed so happily then, fell into my arms, exhausted, your sweet cheeks flushed with joy, and the next day you were gone, my darling, I long to see your face, your eyes, I long for the sound of your laughter, he will crease the pages and throw them into the fire, stiff with guilt that he has not tried to find her since, she lifts her eyes to the clear skies where the kites dance impatiently upon the winds, after many years her imagination has become her refuge, once again, she will rely on the rivulets of fantasy that leach through her consciousness, she will craft the clay of her existence into images of violence, she will sculpt the fragments of her reality into visions of peace, as she had done in her adolescence, her face against a rancid pillow, she would shut out the morning sounds, the cryptic shrieks of the hawkers, the violent slap of wet clothes upon the bathroom floor, she would surround herself in the dense meshes of her fantasies, the pleading eyes of an unknown poet.

Anna lies upon the damp grass, the child upon her, she imagines the long hands that fondle the child's head lying upturned upon the gray earth, swarming with ants, the silken hair crawls lifeless into the dead grass, he bends over her, destroyed by grief, she will watch from a distance, the child's small hand tucked into hers, she is strangely moved by his imagined grief, many years ago she had shed tears not just for herself but for him as she imagined their separation, she had detailed in her mind the depth of his grief, he would look down into the murky depths of the Thames, the Houses of Parliament casting long shadows upon the water, he would look deep into the inky waters for the swirls of her hair, the cloudy dark of her eyes, she would hear in her mind the chimes of Big Ben measuring out his grief, she would watch him roam the English shores, drown his fruitless desire in the roar of the Atlantic, an ocean she had never dreamed that she might see, she saw his dark eyes blinded with sea salt, his black hair blowing stiff in the salt wind, and months later she had stood on the pier at Southend and gazed mournfully at the desolation of seaweed and brine, the feeble waves that moved shyly away, it was only in Cornwall that she satisfied her craving for the dense resonance of the oceans, among the heather, clotted like old blood against the mustard flowers, there, in the ancient air of a deserted tin mine, she had sang with the rain, he had let the moldy raindrops trickle down the nape of his neck, drench the perfume of Anna's lips upon his skin, he does not remember having recollected passion with more pleasure than within the damp walls of a Cornish tin mine, submerged in the tortured sweetness of her song. He rolls over upon the damp heath grass and sits up, it's time we started the decorations, he says, they walk home slowly, the child asleep in his arms.

A s she sifts flour in the kitchen, she can hear the crunch of paper in the dining room, like old bones snapping apart, Anna is folding them into birds and beasts, he sits and watches, mesmerized by the grace of her nimble fingers, a sheet of blue transforms into a mournful pterodactyl, a nonchalant frog, he folds each sheet across and tears off the edge to make it square, he pleats the leftover strips into the accordioned mane of a deformed lion, blindfolded children will move through the afternoon light to pin a tail upon its bare hindquarters. She hears their laughter like distant chimes, her fingers deep in dough, and for the first time, she imagines them making love, she sees them upon the dining table, the paper crushes against their mingled limbs, the soft sheets sigh against her skin, the crude colors of crepe blur with her juices and stain her thighs, her thoughts are interrupted by a sudden silence, are they stunned by their passion, frozen by desire, she stands motionless, the dough thickens around her fingers, the trance is broken by the anguished scream of a bird, like a mirror cracking in the dark, the telephone rings, they are all suddenly out in the hallway, this is how it must have been, she thinks, on the eve of a great war, he picks up the receiver, the tension is broken, it is Trevor, he wants them to come around and celebrate, he has got the job, what job, she does not dare ask, and at his flat, people mill around her, a ponytailed man holds his champagne glass to the child's lips, short gurgles of laughter rise from within her, the man moves closer so that his rancid breath is upon her shoulder, his pupils are dim points in his pale irises, she does not recognize him, his fleshy lips quiver beneath thin nostrils, who are you? he asks in a strange voice, but before she can think of how to answer, he is pulled away by a thin black woman, she has seen her before, at parties, poised like an elegant twig against blank walls, she looks around, in this room she spent her first night in this land, upon this floor they had lain, his arms wrapped around her, and she had woken in the middle of the night, a fearful emptiness within her, she sat with her back pressed against the radiator, from time to time she had looked at her watch whose hands still marked the time of a world she had left behind, it was six in the morning in Calcutta, her father would be stretching his limbs in preparation for his journey to the market, her mother wiping the night sweat from her brow with a stale sari, is boiling the water for his morning tea, her grandmother has been up since four, she has bathed and prayed at her small household shrine, she will touch the blessed flowers to their foreheads, her brother, asleep in her bed, will stir in his sleep as the wet petals graze his skin, ten o'clock now, pitch dark outside, the February cold bit at her toes, Anthony woke, you're jet-lagged, he told her, ten o'clock, her brother swings his cloth bag over his shoulder and leaves for the day, he works the evening shift at the newspaper, so he will not be back until midnight, come back into bed, Anthony said, try and sleep, she turned off the lamp, a muddy paleness was edging in through the curtains, she looked at her watch, eleven o'clock, the girls were rising from their chairs to greet the lecturer, Shakespeare's Tragedies, Tuesdays and Thursdays at eleven, the tinkle of rickshaw bells in the street below bringing housewives to pick up their children from the nursery next door, she had watched them from the window, the children of the rich, tumbling down the dinosaur-shaped slide, clambering onto the swings, an isolated paradise from which they were delivered to their sealed air-conditioned homes, she had pitied them, from the rarefied heights of her classroom window, they would never know what the world held, they would stay curtained in their trivial niches, while she traveled through space and time with Shakespeare, There are more things in heaven and earth, Horatio, than are dreamt of in your philosophy, twelve o'clock, the curtains were pierced by a cold winter light, in Calcutta, the noon sun is caressing the pitted pavements, her mother has delivered the tiffin-carrier loaded with steaming curry and rice to the dark young man whose job it is to take it to her father at his office, she is preparing for her bath, the sun will have warmed the overhead tank, taken the nip out of the water, she suddenly fell into a numb sleep, when she woke, they were sitting in bathrobes drinking scotch, like some breakfast? Trevor asked, his eyes hovering upon her breasts, she drew her bed-clothes up to her chin, yes, please, she said. The child has managed to smear herself with avocado dip, she takes her into the bathroom, the thin black girl is sitting on the edge of the tub, in an intense conversation with a red-haired man in cycling shorts, they apologize and leave, she locks the door, here she had stood confused, on her first morning looking for a shower, the electric shower that spindles its way above is a recent addition, that morning she had washed herself with a tooth glass, the only object she could find that would function as a mug. And Trevor had laid before her two perfect fried eggs, but she had choked as she remembered how much her brother liked fried eggs, how he would scrape at her plate for tiny drops of congealed yolk, and last year, she had fed him to her heart's content, doused the smell of alcohol upon his breath with rich spices, mounds of rice, the nibbles at the tapas bar had not satisfied his tropical appe-tite, that night after the play, when she had sat by him and watched him eat the leftovers she had warmed, she had wished he had, instead of attempting to flirt with Anna, noticed the tense desire between her and Anthony, she had hoped he would express horror at her predicament, the dim belief had existed within her benumbed consciousness that somehow he would deliver her from the distant pain that jerked her awake on sad gray mornings, but he had wiped the lentil steam off his thick glasses and asked her to turn on the Japanese film on BBC2, and so she had lowered the volume and waited for him to finish his food, her thoughts swamped by shrill oriental whispers, and he sat with his eyes fixed upon the screen while she cleared the dishes, his soiled fingers stiff in the air, and she had remembered how, when they were young, they had often sat talking at the dining table until the curry dried upon their fingers, like flakes of insect wings.

When she emerges from the bathroom, they are standing together at the door looking around for her, she picks up the child and moves towards them, she stands in the mist of their champagne-thickened lust, why don't you stay here awhile, he says, we'll just drive over to pick something up at Anna's, we won't be long, she smells the gorged impatience upon his breath, I'd rather come, she says, I'm not feeling very well, a mesh of fine fishbones crushes in the air between them, all right then, he says, dully, come along, while she is burrowing for her coat under the pile upon Trevor's bed, the ponytailed man whispers in her ear, you will never forget me, she smiles and turns away, will she remember him, in the quiet menace of tropical rain-clouds, will she remember the fetid sweetness of stale cham-pagne upon her ear, the trembling lips, the thin trouser legs flapping upon wiry thighs, the chipped fingernails waving in the lank air, or should she perhaps let them leave, and beckon to him with her eyes, submit to the stench of his wild breath in the stalled lift, she trembles at the depth of her imagination, she stops at the door to look back, he has fallen asleep upon the mound of overcoats, his pullover riding up to reveal a taut corpse-colored belly like the underside of a diseased fish, she makes her way to the front door, they walk down the dim stairs into the pleasant October afternoon, she feels she should have stayed back, she has intensified their excitement with the obstacle of her presence, his shallow breaths fall like the slap of parchment upon the windscreen, Anna's eyes are a frozen green like the colored ices that their father would buy them, that they sucked out of polythene bags on tropical fairgrounds, waiting for their turn on the hand-churned Ferris wheel, Anna opens the heavy wooden door to her flat, the aroma of turpentine, she is face to face with a large canvas of herself and the child, painted in Anna's mother's garden, this summer, her face veiled by a waterfall of hair, the child's head upon her lap, they are drowning in flowers, wild masses of foliage tower over them, menacing tulips hover against their flesh, splashes of a mordant ocher edge the darkness of her hair, and somewhere within, a deep translucent blue spells peace, she is suddenly overwhelmed by the wealth of color, so this is the backdrop to their furious lovemaking, she has not been here in a long time, but she is disappointed, no giveaway sock has to be hastily concealed, the smell of fresh lust does not rise to greet her from the inkstained fleece on the bed, instead the aroma of fermenting newspaper drifts across from a vat of papier mâché against the wall, the needle jumps on the record, Anna is searching through a pile of books, okay, we can go now, she says, I've found it, she waves a thin book, *Advanced Paper Aircraft Construction,* he laughs, and she wonders if it is true that she really came for this book, or has the pretext for an afternoon of quick love somehow flourished into a new string of ideas for the party, we can go now, says Anna, stretching her long limbs into the still air, but she wishes to linger, to tread upon the protrusions of dried oil paint upon the dusty floor, to gaze into the shadowy corners of the lofty ceiling that take her back to the old people's home on Lower Circular

Road that she and Sharmila visited regularly, her brother thought it typically bourgeois, a game they played, dressing in stiff white saris, their hair pulled demurely back, they would set off, to lay their young hands upon gnarled Anglo-Indian arms, the last forlorn dregs of a vanished past, families that had returned to Europe while they were left behind, the shriveled Austrian who had never seen Austria spoke bitterly of a happy childhood in the Himalayan foothills, a husband who had died without leaving her money or children, she had always returned shaken, how would it be to live in a world without a soul to call your own, the gray eyes, dim with age, moistened under the cobwebbed vaults of the ceiling, a spectacled nun asked Sharmila, would your mother like to do a sponsored dinner this year, or would she rather just give us a check? Lonely eyes would follow them down the long verandas and turn again to the indifferent skies above Lower Circular Road, once a trench to protect against the fierce Marathas, now a river of contorted traffic, spitting thick fumes of raw fuel into the air, they must have eaten through her bones by now, the little old lady who would never see Austria, instead, Moni had stood in the shadow of the fountains and wondered where within these streets, many many years ago, a young man and his wife had packed their bags to leave for an exotic land, a bourgeois pastime, her brother had called it, think of the thousands of old people who die on the pavements every day, who does anything for them, perhaps, when she goes back, she can work for a charity, expunge her sins of having lived in a land of plenty by devoting her life to the poor, the diseased, the hungry, she can see herself, clothed in dull white, soothing a sick child, a new energy seizes her, that is what she must do, it is clear to her now, that is how she will spend the rest of her life, she sits up on the bed, yes, let's go, then, she says, there is still plenty to be done, she casts a last long look at the room, the painting of her and the child, she had not noticed that Anna had painted little white flowers in her hair, like strangled stars.

She will give her life to the city that she left behind, so many years ago, before its wooing of her was complete, she had crept away, before she might have shared the deathly pain of dying desire with its forlorn streets, before the sting of a forgotten lust might have sent her stumbling into the dawn shroud of greasy mist that lay over the lake where her father took his morning walk, she had walked too, every morning, one summer, with a cousin who was dying for the love of a young man who came at dawn to row upon the rancid waters, they never saw him, although her cousin would seize her hand in wild panic every time a shell glided by, she had married him, two years later, the groom's family gave a reception at the rowing club, and sitting on the bank in the pleasant November evening, she had wondered whether her cousin would ever confess how she had hunted from these very shores for a glimpse of his face, whether they would laugh in helpless delight, watching the moonlight sink into the dark water, she had wondered why it was only for her that love remained a dream, and when love came, she had not shared it with the city, as the others had, weeping upon the heavy grass by the lake, spreading their sighs into the firm moonlight, she had closeted her passion within herself, drawn the corset strings tight upon her desire, she had not let loose her despair upon the vile pavements, tainted her sorrows with blood and dung, had instead perplexed her college friends with her silence, they watched in the weeks that passed after the dread night of fireworks when he had buried his haunted lips upon her trembling mouth, upon her dusk hair, they watched her in the days that followed with curious, troubled eyes, for between them a veil of glass had descended, she had not come to them as others had with fearful details of a first caress, they could not fathom what had passed between her and the tall foreigner who waited every day, after classes, smoking violently at the gate, they touched her with tender affection, when she sat, often, with her head buried in her arms upon a desk, they stroked her hair, patted her cold hands, but they did not dare ask, not even Sharmila, although, with her, she spoke sometimes in short enigmatic spurts, painful word games, that would end in sharp silence, she liked very much to feel their hands upon her, cool against the lingering embers of his hungry palms, pressing deep into her arms, stroking frenzy into her wrists, the wounds of his lips were still fresh upon her, at night she would fearfully draw her lips into her mouth and taste smoke and blood, run her fingers endlessly through her hair, charred from his hands, she craved the smell of her mother, of warm cotton and turmeric, but her mother had not held her in years, and in these weeks a deep unease had condensed between them, even though, when he came, she would hardly ever emerge from her bedroom, her brother never summoned her anymore to entertain the Englishman, teased her no longer that he had come, naturally, to see her, and she was not commanded now to take out the tea, to help roll dough for snacks. One day he brought her a bilingual copy of Rimbaud, so that he might have some excuse to ask for her, she came forth from behind the cruel curtain, sat like dry wood in the chair beside him, but she could not avoid his eyes anymore when she noticed, to her surprise, when he held the book out to her his hands were shaking, and raising her eyes to him she saw that the hard shadows of his deep eyes were diffuse with pain, for a week had passed since the evening when he had first reached out, under skies of fire, to touch her, a week had passed and she had hidden away, she had not come to any of the rehearsals, none of the film shows, even the classical music performance at the indoor stadium, she had avoided him, and so, one afternoon, he had picked up a copy of Rimbaud from the stall under the Grand Hotel, and taken a minibus to their home, and in a voice that slithered among the silver afternoon shadows, he had asked to see her, and when her eyes lifted to him as he gave her the book he had held them in tight sorrow, until her wooden limbs relaxed, and instead of rising to leave, she had stayed, until it was time for her class at the Alliance Française, he had left with her, insisted on a taxi, and in the half-darkness, he had seized her hands, I must kiss you again, I have to kiss you, tell me where we can go so that I can kiss you, and she had shuddered as, despite herself, images of hotel rooms floated dangerously, the unoccupied flat where a friend's fiancé had once taken them, his uncle's flat, that the family would not occupy until his uncle retired, he had explained, and after an hour of laughter and teasing, they had left them there to the white-washed echoes of their love, they still met within those empty rooms, and shutting her eyes she tried to crush the overwhelm-ing desire to be there with him, alone, in the bare shadows, a furious urge boiled within her to see where those desperate kisses might lead, and how would her flesh respond, stunned as it was now in his violent hands, she shuddered and turned away, oh, the clean lines of the uncurtained windows called, tomorrow classes would resume at her college, she need only ask her friend for the key, but the indignity repelled her, and the horrible fear that in the fulfillment of his desire would be the end of their love, that the bare walls would mock the empty shell of their passions, once his lips had gorged upon her, sucked her dry, she began to cry, slowly, and, strangely, he found comfort in her tears, for her stormy gasps carried the exhaustion of lovemaking, stroking her wet cheeks, he asked, will you marry me, please, you must marry me, she shook her head, I won't go away, he said, almost gaily, until you agree to marry me, he smiled, I won't leave this city without you, and the city had stared balefully, penitently, through the murky windows of the taxi, the dim evening lights had blinked fearfully, and when the tired darkness edged in to soothe her, she had flinched, snatched herself away from the shadowy fingers, she had been too proud then, to share her pain with the city, would the city allow her now to tend its sores, the city, whose tired blistered nipples she had pushed aside with disdainful lips, for within her a great longing has risen to hold to her all its starving children, to wipe the weak saltless sweat from their brittle limbs, deliver them from the adult prison of reality, undressing the child for bed, she looks in horror at the hurricane of toys that lie scattered about the room, so many toys, if only they could take them all with them, to give to the slum children, or even her own cousins, she remembers a day, many years ago, when, in a fit of beneficence, she had given away all her dolls, even the foreign dolls that her aunt brought from Canada, to their maid's daughters, and then, later that day, as she was leaving for music school, her eyes fell upon a face among the group of ragged children that played on the pavement outside their home, an unfamiliar child, fingering the nylon hair of one of the dolls, her face seemed clouded with a dense longing for the pretty doll, to hold its stiff limbs close to her, feel its rough hair upon her sleepy face, the clink of its hinged lids as it lay with her to sleep, the peace of the glass blue eyes as she shook it awake in the morning light, but some other, possessive little hands tugged at the doll, reluctantly the child let it slip from her hands, and the sweet satisfaction of the morning drained away leaving bitter foam, like the head of Guinness into which Anthony had once, many years ago, coaxed her to dip her tongue, he calls now, from downstairs, we'll be stopping by at the off-license for some beer, do you need anything for tomorrow? For some reason, they always insist on beer with Tandoori food, she has never understood why, they will have takeaway Tandoori for dinner tonight, because there is no time to cook, and they will have beer, and later, when he takes her back home, their bitter breath will mingle, on their last night of unfettered love, for no more will he smite her flesh with the uninterrupted desire of one for whom a child will wake to soothe the roughness on his lips with a small soft cheek, and the sweet tang of deceit, half deceit, will have been crushed indigo by her absence, and yet perhaps, at least for a time, they will revel in the ecstasy of a deserted home, as they might have glutted their desire upon the blank white walls of a vacant flat, many years ago, if she had not been so shaken by the tawdriness of the image, and if night had not fallen like dusty feathers to hide the dark of his eyes, soft, like broken eggshells, with love. Perhaps, for a time, his lover will wander in this house, naked, burning milk in her saucepans, perhaps they will make love to the smell of burnt milk, perhaps the exhilaration of freedom will overwhelm the loss of peace and the small pleasures in the contortions of deceit, and although she might, on some days, catch her breath at the sound of his weeping, lay down her brush upon the kitchen table, for she will have, surely, by then, set up a studio in the kitchen, the tiles caking paint, hard dry knobs of paint on the varnished pine, she will lay down her brush and creep softly upstairs, and there she might stand in the doorway of the child's room and watch him drown the bed in tears, she would stand at this doorway, smelling of turpentine and thick juicy oil, and his semen, she will watch his great shoulders heave, and then, perhaps the delicious sensation of trespassing will crumple within her, but briefly, for he will surely turn his aching eyes upon her, and they will fall upon this very floor in paroxyms of desire sharpened by pain, the juices of their passion will mingle with turpentine into the soft threads of this carpet, that just this morning, in blind habit, she has vacuumed with Alpine Glade. And if it is so, she thinks suddenly, a clear cold thought piercing a curtain of pain, if it is so, what will it matter to her, for she will be far away, embracing the poor and the hungry in a city that she once disdained, preferring the darkness, soft as crushed eggshell, in his eyes, he, who could never have loved her more than the brave pitted streets had loved her, the broad humid shadows of tired trees in lonely parks, the dull membranes of a tormented river, dragging through eons of alluvium to meet its ancient love, the sea. What will it matter to her, if he chooses simply to forget her, if the loss of his child shakes him only like an intermittent fever, she will never know, tonight is her last opportunity to see him suffer, it is the last night of pain, and of pleasure, the child is breathing peacefully, the doorbell rings, they are back, she pries open the aluminum foil with fish knives, and Anna produces from a bag a bottle of champagne, we thought we might try this, since it is a sort of special night, it's from India, she smiles, the exotic Shiraz grape, it would seem, is outdoing the splendid Australian Chardonnay, she tumbles in small laughter, so it will be champagne then, even if it sits like rusty cumin upon her tongue, Anthony and Anna find it quite passable, those are the words they use, and even though it stings like raw fennel upon her palate, she takes a second glass.

And if he were to write of this night, as indeed he might in the years to come, he would have started by remarking, as he did to Anna driving her home, on how strangely loquacious she had been, that night, how unfettered her laughter, for he would surely turn this tragedy into a source of dense inspiration, as he had mutilated the miserable circumstances of his sister's death into a tender short story, his only work that had found its way into print, one that he had begun to write, he had confessed, many years before, in Calcutta, hence the sudden interjections of red oleander, sad michelia, shivering marigolds, and then for years it had gathered dust, and then, one summer, in a rented cottage on Brittany's battered shores, he had fished from his briefcase the yellowed remains of the story he had begun upon the mosaicked veranda of a grand colonial house, many years ago in Calcutta, on a still tropical evening, he had scratched furiously upon the thick whorled sheets that Amrita's mother had found for him, written desperately to quell the first twinges of a bold despair that had overcome him that afternoon as he sat talking to Moni of his childhood, for her eyes had colored deep with a different emotion when he told her quietly of his sister's death, in faint horror, he had allowed himself to craft the details to suit her girlish nightmares, and that evening, with the sickly sweet smell of jasmine thick about him, he had retched the soiled memories that he had concealed from her upon the turbid sheets, and yet there had been a powerful poetry in the distance of their experiences, he had looked at her across a windy ravine, heady with the scent of a torrent of emotion that was his alone, there had been poetry, and in Brittany, his head upon her knee as he read his manuscript, not for her ears, but for Anna's, late-summer evening, quiet sea shadow, she had mused hesitatingly on whether the dark uncomprehending eyes that weaved in and out of the narrative were not hers, but he spoke of them with a passion that was so alien to the imperturbable affection in which he smothered her now that she did not dare presume, his voice rose, with proud dense passion, for how could I love you, my hands full of strawberries, if I had not left myself behind on a narrow bed, among white walls and the smells of thunder, he folded the manuscript triumphantly, and rose from the couch to meet the eyes of his lover, eyes misted with hunger, for they had not made love in a while, not since he had pushed her up against the wooden front door of her flat, bags packed, and the two of them waiting in the car downstairs, double-parked, in furious gusts he made love to her, in deft and rapid delight, and then, for a few precious seconds, watched his satisfied breath stain the pitted whorls upon the door, while she readjusted her clothes, he took down her bags, tweaked the child's nose through the car window, a week and a half had passed since then, and he had slept every night at her side, writing late into the night, she would fall asleep to the sound of his excited breath, and during the day, playing with the child upon the dead grass under his window, she would listen for his breath, the forgotten sounds of a dissatisfied desire, that had fallen in such delicious pain upon her ears, many years ago, among the festival din, the dark steam of his lust, college gates flaking rust upon his clenched fingers, when will I see you again, and one morning, she watched his terrible eyes recede, smudged in ink, she stood for a while at the gate, and then, glancing desperately up at the row of girls that watched her from the balcony, she had turned and without a word walked out again into the street, he had turned by then, walking blindly, it seemed to her, into the glassy morning, she followed quietly, determined that if he did not see her, she would turn back, but near the corner paan shop he stopped to light a cigarette with the smoldering coil nailed upon the bright blue boards, and raising the snaked coil to his lips, he turned, and seeing her, took the cigarette from his glad lips and threw it in a strangely local gesture upon a pile of garbage on the road, frightening a foraging crow, and with the coil still in his fingers he came towards her, as if he might brand her with his passion, press the burning butt to her palm, as in the flimsy Turgenev paperback that a schoolfriend had never returned, she stood against the college walls, trying to cement remembered fragments of the story, walls encrusted with election campaigns of many decades, she leaned back against a purple hammer and sickle, and letting the coil fall from his hands, he came and stood by her, eyes trembling like young, liquid night, the darkness upon the edge of a dream, glass clouds raced upon the listless sky, the streets were threadbare, penitent, crouching away from the strange vapors that encircled her, they wandered all morning in the waxed silence of the museum, deep in honeyed gloom, the heavy amber that precedes an inevitable storm, and then suddenly, tracing circles in the thin dust upon a horizontal glass cabinet, he began to speak, in thick swirling sentences that packed into her mind like compressed cotton wool, let us hold this moment forever, he was saying, for I have never felt such grand pain, she felt really that he was speaking to himself rather than her, clearing circles in the glass to find the reflection of his own sleepless eyes, among the faded jewels of defeated kings, speak to me, he looked up at her, speak to me, please, tell me how you feel, his anguished pleas folded into her, I must get back to college, she said, insulated from his despair by the weight of his words, they walked slowly back, but at the gates they lingered again, and then seizing her in his tormented hands he pulled her away as the bell chimed the end of a lecture, before the open corridors swarmed again with young women, they walked quickly away, in the skies above, a china glass outline of the moon, the moon has lost her memory, he said, turning to her, smiling for the first time in the day, for the smell of victory lurked in the stiff smoky air, or at least, he continued, she has lost her head, her sense of time, the moon, she looked upon the penciled scabs upon its pale face, stretched like milk upon the winter sky, they picked their way up the broken pavements on Free School Street, shall we eat something, he asked, gesturing towards a small Chinese restaurant where they had come often, after college, to watch their desire curl in hot wisps from large kettles of chimney soup, let the strong steam settle into their eyes, they climbed the stairs into the lamplit interior, a cold dampness clung to them as they retreated to a corner table, they asked for green tea, his hands shook with the small cups, scattering pale warm drops, on his unshaven chin, shadows of manhood were deepening your saheb, her brother had remarked jokingly, a few months ago, before the matter had transcended the realm of ridicule, your saheb, when disheveled, bears an unfortunate resemblance to the alcoholic heros of Sarat

· 117 ·

Chandra Chatterjee, whose watery prose he despised, snorting in exasperation, on rainy afternoons, when she curled up on the divan with one of his novels, their mother had purchased his collected works from a salesman, many years ago, in the dim light of Chinese lamps, his dark hair scattered over his forehead, he did indeed look as if he might drink himself to death, as if the lukewarm tea that he sipped quietly might be laced with aromatic poison, but his eyes had lost the sweet desperation of that morning, for he knew already, as the boy slid bowls of Manchurian chicken upon the scratched glass tabletop, he knew then, that within her the mist had melted, that her mind was the slate gray of storm, the last lamp had been quenched under winds that she could no longer hold back, when he saw her again that evening, a hard blue line had been drawn between him and her life in this uncorseted city, dusk-veiled, whose entrails lay open to the sky, then, ten years ago, as men burrowed into its flesh, and the excavated arteries lay foul with disease, trains rattled in those caverns today, where a friend's brother had drowned earlier that year, on a dare, a bright, impetuous boy, the city had swallowed him, she had been shaken badly for it had been clear to her always that the boy had worshiped her, even loved her, with the awkward desire of an adolescent, and she had crushed his fancies with the characteristic dignity of an older sister's friend, years later, watching on television the depthless torment of a young boy in postwar Germany, one who loved a woman, many years older, who might have been his brother's wife, her mind would convulse in unfamiliar pain for the ungainly boy, who had choked to death upon the mildewed innards of the city, whom she had bruised so gravely by turning away from his penetrating eyes, through hard window bars he would stare darkly, studying on the veranda, while they, happy college girls, draped themselves upon the massive bed in their only room, where her friend and her brother lived with their mother, a schoolteacher, and a party worker, they rarely saw her, for she came home late, although the very first time that Moni had come to their home, she had come home early, sweating with a deep fever, and Moni had sat by her side, loosening her blouse, wiping her brow, where the sweat sheen glimmered dark, while her friend ran to fetch a doctor, and where was a doctor to be found, in the heavy silence of a summer afternoon. Yet her friend, ignoring her mother's protests, ran down the chipped stairs into the immobile afternoon, and was gone for an interminable hour, while the woman continued to mumble, searching helplessly for hot breath, that she did not need a doctor, she did not like doctors, and Moni loosened the tight cords of her petticoat, fumbled under her back with the cruel hooks of her yellowed brassiere, her back like wet charcoal, she lay almost senseless, and the boy, standing at the foot of the bed, one hand tightly clenching the rough wood of the bednet frame, had given his young heart to her, and so on happier days, when they sat upon the bed, playing cards, or weaving tales, half-holiday afternoons, he would gaze upon her from behind thick iron bars, and she would quietly change her position upon the vast bed, and he would be forced to turn his eyes away, towards the muddy pond beyond, the stale reflections of tired summer light upon its stagnant waters, a mangy mongrel might limp by, his bamboo chair would scrape upon the cement floor, in the afternoon shadows, his splintered form, what does "elute" mean? he demanded of them once, yes, like "elude," only with a "t," who knows, his sister curled her mouth in irritation, look it up in the dictionary, and despite herself, despite the deep desire to ignore the arrogant, yet so pathetic eyes, she commanded him to read the whole sentence, but the context was hopelessly scientific, he shut his crumbling text with a triumphant bang, how can you expect us to know these scientific words, his sister growled at him, but it's just a verb, he protested, and you are all students of English, and later that day, she searched in the *Concise Oxford* for "elute," her index finger trembling inexplicably, running down the page, and elute, that strangely melodious word, which the boy had flattened under his hard tongue, elute, like the brush of dead wings upon a harp, elute, like the long, low call of a lovesick bird, elute meant to wash out (a substance) by the action of a solvent, as in chromatography, from the Latin, elutus, and from elute came eluent, a solvent used for eluting, eluent, that should have been a quality of mermaid voices, an adjective for the sigh of sea foam upon harsh rock, the scream of an eagle whose nestling suffocates upon fish she has buried too deep, too deep into its throat, eluent, committed now to some pale spiteful chemical, glorified soap, and the boy had died some days later, plunging into the intestines of the city, on a frivolous dare, she held his mother's hands, stone hands, tearless, dead eyes, and that winter, when he sat back silent after weaving the story of his sister's death against the contours of her young gloom, she wiped her eyes, and told him falteringly of what she called her only close experience of death, he was like a brother to me, she told him, and he believed her, for he had seen how eagerly brothers and sisters were shared, and overwhelmed by the horror of death, she had forgotten, almost, that he had loved her, years later, the adolescent agony of a curly-haired German boy, thrashing upon a church organ, brought back memories, soft splinters of dead wood, that in the stillness of a tropical winter had been submerged in the darkness of death, still fresh upon her, as he twisted the fragments of his old pain into a tale of peace and beauty, and that evening, in the shade of jasmine, he had bled the last shards of his misery upon virgin paper, and as he wrote, the despair that he had not been able to tell her all acquired the velvet edges of a cosmic solitude, I am alone, he thought, intoxicated with lust, I will always be alone, my fingers encrusted with cold ink, caressing silk silence, our love, he was not afraid then that the wordless spaces between them would petrify, for he burned with overwhelming desire, cooling his cheeks upon the broad thigh of a marble statue at the top of the banister while the household slept, he drank in the immense solitude of the universe, I am alone, will ever be alone, in Brittany, his head on her knee, he spoke of dark eyes drawing further and further away, like stars in the wake of pale cosmic wind, like galaxies spiraling far into an endless dark, he spoke of a painter trying to capture on canvas a smile, before it faded into morning, into silence, our love, sweet silence, I have never heard her talk so much, he now tells Anna, ghostly pale in intermittent lamplight, I have never known her to be so voluble, never, she nods silently, gloomy almost, a little jealous, he dares think, for she had unleashed an exotic aroma, suddenly from within her, strange myths, and violet memories, hothouse flowers, Trevor would have delighted in her tonight, he says chuckling, Trevor, she had called him the moon of a moonless night, still there was something pathetic, hysterical about her uncharacteristic loquacity, his heart fills with sudden compassion.

They told her to wrap the surprise in Pass the Parcel, layer after layer, she encased it in discarded sheets, parcels within parcels, will they lie embedded within each other forever, she wonders as she releases the attic door, she climbs the accordion ladder, she is within the dark vaults of their past.

How strangely full of sad tales she has been, he thinks, as the traffic light turns a rapid amber, she told them how during the Naxalite unrest of the early seventies, she had woken to find all her flower pots smashed, and her wonderful flowers, rich marigolds, trampled under heavy boots, the police had taken away the boy upstairs, she had been fond of him, he always gave her chocolates, hard toffee outside, and a soft melted center, how careful she had been with detail, mesmerized in private recollection, she was scared, she told them, of biting too hard and draining the soft center, for that was the best part, and what became of the boy, Anna had asked impatiently, he never came back, she said, they must have shot him, released him and then put a bullet through his head as he walked shakily towards the prison gates, towards freedom, an unaccustomed hardness penetrating her voice, it must have been the champagne, Anna says.

She sits with her hands thick in photographs, boxes of photographs that she must leave behind, or should she fill these empty suitcases with these papery memories, what are they worth to her now, for these are memories that have been banished from the warm corners of their home, they have not found shelter within the flimsy sleeves of the photograph albums that line the walls of their bedroom, the girl, growing from a wrinkled peevish bundle into plump contented childhood, faded prints of their wedding, still a curiosity, to Anna especially, who never failed, while they dressed perhaps for some occasion, in her bedroom, to pry open the congealed pages bound in polythene Kashmiri sunset, another hilarious wedding gift, these are brilliant, she said every time, you look gorgeous, see, she would say to the child, floating by for bedtime kisses, see, doesn't your mother look like a princess, the doorbell would ring always sending shivers up her spine, for it would be the sitter, some stranger she must trust with her child, she sits with her hands deep in a box of photographs, those that had never graced the sooty pages of the albums he kept downstairs, to gaze fondly at his artistry, to show, with a wonderful, open pleasure that still drew her, sometimes, to him, that smile, neither modest nor proud, with which he displayed his photographs to his friends, but these he had brushed aside, unwanted children, perhaps she should take them with her, fill her suitcases with unfocused memories, she tips out a box of glossy black-and-white prints, they sink into the insulation in the unboarded sleeves of the attic, the naked bulb casts an acid light upon them, they are all studies of her hands, her hands folded, clenched, spread help-lessly flat, upon a sheet of white blotting paper, her hands meet-ing in prayer, fingers meeting in a cage, fingers crossed like a valley of swords, her hands with a leaf, a dry leaf of a forgotten autumn, caressing, crushing, ripping, and then, between the rip in the leaf, an eye, her eye, she lets them drop and empties another box over them, these are of Anna, of her lifting her hair off the swan curve of her neck, his motor drive had split this gesture into a million fragments, she strews them over the insu-lation, one of the photographs takes an impossible cartwheel and floats down onto the corridor carpet.

This torrent of anecdotes began, he thinks, maneuvering round the Marble Arch, it all began when Anna mentioned, raising a morsel of lamb tikka to her lovely lips, that the crotch-ety old concierge at the Bethlehem had kicked the bucket, and to their surprise, she had said, in my language, we would say he has picked snake gourd, to mean someone has died, and then she had added, smiling, and Trevor we would call the moon of a moonless night, which is what we say of someone we do not see very often.

Fields of rape, and warm thick mustard, rinsed tortured gray, he has captured the raucous green of the tropics in a matte of gray, black clouds hang over a flooded tropical garden, the crumbling stone statuettes drowning in blind mud, a gray sheet of rain, and he would have turned his wet eyes to the damp marble halls, the tender shadows of her face weaving like raw wine through his turgid mind, the gray lions choke upon the dead petals that the sea of black filth leaves upon their stoic nostrils, they stare in blind blurred grief through the curtain of rain, most of these photographs are hopelessly indistinct, for his eyes, keen with new exhilaration, had seen much more than his camera lens, the cold precise objectivity was gnawed by a sense of the unreal, for he felt on that day that he had penetrated the very spirit of life in this city, the very essence of their culture had been revealed to him in the few dense hours he had gazed upon the rain-swollen curve of her mouth, this was what he had come to discover, to feel, the inebriation of tropical rain upon his skin, the sensual exchange of poetry on a thunderous evening, oh, if he could only draw his lips through the velvet valley of her hair, his experience of the tropics would be complete, if he could only once graze the succulence of her lips, a manservant brings him a plate of sliced mango, he bites gratefully into the fragrant flesh, the thick juices soothe his throat, inexplicably parched in contrast to the saturation of his skin, his rain-raw eyes, Amrita's mother-in-law emerges from the damp interior, shivering, he asks her for water, she smiles, we say that water should never be taken after fruit, why, he asked Moni tonight, remembering this piece of curious advice as she regaled them with amusing proverbs, and she had ascribed it to nothing more than the unlucky phonic resemblance between the words for fruit and water in Bengali, although she admitted that a glass of water after bananas always made her a little queasy, and like a tremor of warm music the image quivered within him, of the old lady smoothing back her damp hair, in the long dusky veranda, he had held his sticky fingers out to the rain, and told her, I cannot tell you how happy I feel today, he held out both hands through the grille, the woman shuddered, in this rain, how can you feel so ecstatic in this rain, she asked, this rain is ravishing, he told her, this rain is like an inexhaustible torrent of love, an indefatigable—he stopped, he did not want to embarrass her, she shook her head, you are mad, she said affectionately, and disappeared indoors, leaving him to continue his panegyric silently, the rain is like an indefatigable lover, he thought, penetrating all crevices of thought, numbing all sensation but that of its incessant beat upon the ears, a dull drum in the blood, the flesh swells with its juices, but the insides are parched, dry, dehydrated, and as he muses, the wind turns, sharp and sudden, and his face is caressed by sharp rain wound, he rushes to protect his camera, hurries indoors, the servants are rapidly shutting the doors and windows, how long can this go on, laments their mistress, my rheumatism will kill me, but inside, although the rain vapor hangs in ethereal swirls about the heavy mahogany, the polished teak is misted with the breath of rain, all else is intact, unperturbed, unlike the household where he has spent the previous night, where he had woken to turmoil, the slap of wet feet, rainwater lapping dangerously outside the door, in the corridor outside the bathroom, a tin bucket gaped anxiously at a widening circle of damp in the ceiling, the mother fretted and fumed, the father complained to him about the inundation of the market, wiping rain slime off his legs, his wife brought him a tub of hot water to soak his aching feet, that evening, in his diary, Anthony wrote, the rain emphasizes socioeconomic divisions, sealed out from the homes of the rich, seeping slowly into the homes of the middle class, and grinding the homes of the poor to fine mud, all that was blurred and baked dry by the pacific sun, he hesitated, wondering how to write of her, so that, later, when he burrowed into his past, these memories would be sheathed in light honey, not discolored by dry-boned declarations of lust, that would never withstand the test of time, this he knew, that he must cast the desire of the afternoon in dense abstraction, as time would have wrought from the supernatants of unrecorded recollection, if he is to preempt nostalgia, he must weave his own ambrosial haze, with words, words, words that will not dry in the damp sweeps of the mournful ceiling fan, his brain, beaten to pulp by the wooden rhythm of the rain, squeezes watery phrases, and so he withdraws from the embrace of the blank white pages, before his mood of elation is flooded over, before his supreme sense of fulfillment is blotted blue on the sodden sheets, there is always the night, and the filters of dream, that will sharpen his prose for the morning, and then he will sit, in the lemon light of the dying rainstorm, to write of her eyes, sipping Orange Pekoe from Victorian china, if only he might brush those heavy lids with his eager tongue, taste, once and for all, the beauty of this rotting paradise.

She remembers how his hands trembled as he reached for his keys, tonight, in an excitement that was beyond lust, how his hands murmured at Anna's hips while he steadied her as she hung balloons, stiff pterodactyls, luminous salamanders, she has swathed the rice-paper shades in colored chains, tilted fluted peacock tails from the moldings, the room now resembles one of her collages, in one corner, the paper planes dangle, the *Advanced Paper Aircraft Construction* has proved to be a gold mine, split nosecone darts rub noses with super loopers, and jump jets, although he did have some trouble with the advanced undercarriage on the glider, and Anna had to leave her to slice the jelly oranges while she helped him, her deft fingers moved like magic, and there was the advanced undercarriage, and she had told them, all we ever made, in India, was boats, to sail in the muddy drains, blotting drainwater, they would collapse and sink, unless some lucky child's uncle had picked out for him the silver foil from a cigarette packet, those sailed long, so long that, finally, in impatience, they would poke it with a stick, or pelt it with stones, once, in a holiday home in Digha, they had thrown stones at slothful toads, lingering on the slopes of the shallow basin of a disused fountain, until rebuked by the son of the family with whom they shared the sprawling bungalow, a dreamy college boy, who dug in the sand for ant-lion larvae that tickled deliciously on one's palm, he had clasped her little hands in his, and asked her to consider the unbearable agony of the unfortunate amphibians, would you like to be pelted with sharp stones, he had asked, it is her first clear memory of guilt, she told them, but he cannot picture her throwing stones at frogs, his mind balks, yet again, remembering her words, we hit them with stones, and they would slip into the pit of slime, and crawl out again, to be struck down, by us, he cannot see them, brother and sister, crouching over the pitted basin, aiming stones at frogs, he surrenders to the inflexibility of his imagination, sighing as he pulls into a parking space at the corner.

She packs hastily, first the child's clothes, a few favorite toys, she shoves the suitcase under the child's bed, her own clothes she throws in haphazardly, she looks around, there is nothing else, nothing else she would like to take, her hands hover over the photograph albums, she is torn between the certainty that the child will demand these, when she is older, loving memories of the hours she has spent poring over her own childhood albums edge against the unbearable conviction that it would be an act of ultimate cruelty to deprive him of them, the bedroom radio suddenly bursts into being, as it has done every night, at this ungodly hour, ever since last Sunday, when he came to her suddenly, while she was watching the BBC evening news, he came to her, dripping sleep, I must rest, he told her, wake me at midnight, and she had set the alarm, in case, seduced by the dry gray feathers of insomnia, she should forget, forget to wake him, but he had only groaned as she reached over to silence the raptures of a late-night sermon, and tonight it turns on again to somber scripture, and the woman, Eve, he condemned to crawl on her belly upon the earth, to bring forth children in great pain, and yet to desire her husband, who would rule over her, she snaps shut the locks on the suitcase. Is it true that she will never see him again, will it be easier if on his way back he crashes into a lamppost and breaks his skull, Anna would come to live with her then, if he were to die, if the doorbell were to ring now, ominous, hollow, they would come to rush her to the hospital where he would be lying, his hair clotted with blood, under sheeted shroud, and tomorrow, she would unpack the guilty suitcases, throw the clothes back into the empty wardrobes, and the Lord told Adam that he must eat the plants of the fields, she turns off the radio, will she never see him again, a noise downstairs stiffens panic within her like frothed egg white, she lifts the suitcase from the bed and locks it quickly within her empty wardrobe, but it is only the wind, knocking briefly, he is still deep within his lover, languidly inhaling the dregs of an excruciating lust, with the drenching of his senses came the elusive image of her pelting sullen frogs, on this he muses quietly, a cheek upon Anna's shoulder, as he watches the warmth rise from her unsatisfied skin and fade into the miasma of thin turpentine, he finds amused satisfaction in the idea that tonight making love to Anna he has thought of her, although not with the despairing lust for Anna that he had inflicted upon her flesh, one moonlit night, many years ago, in a valley of dry lavender, this curious convolution diverts him as she pushes him away and rises from the bed, and so life will fold in upon itself, he murmurs, he can hear her showering, and he longs for the sound of rain.

Her head spins a little as she moves down the stairs, her mind is in the tortured realm where wakefulness has fed on rarified wakefulness, she will not sleep, she thinks, she will not sleep, tonight, though fragile webs of thought might dissolve like weak fishbones, under ponderous fatigue, though gray-feathered memories will lull her with soft fringes, still she will not sleep, and the gray feathers will pack within her mind, cram painfully against her skull, like being buried from the inside, her mind trembles with fear, clods of earth will fall inside her, choking her, burying her nose, her eyes, beat against her eardrums, she sits down suddenly upon the stairs, but he must not see her there, when he turns the key in the door, he must not see her upon the steps, she rises again, wanders into the darkness, she must leave, if only he were to die tonight, spill his brains out upon the prostituted tarmac, cast life in a finality of sea-blue slate, the underside of whale, a finality that she cannot confer upon her existence, not even by leaving, her impotence fills her with deep tears that, instead of fanning like milk sheen upon her cheeks, run alkaline-harsh down the back of her parched throat, if he were to die tonight and relieve her of the petty charades that will crown her day tomorrow, then his memory would dry upon her like the spent sunlight in the veins of autumn leaves, instead it will fester, deep, rotting green, bitter juices rising within her on unfinished summer afternoons, the silence, stiff, soiled parchment, spread socketless across empty rooms.

A nna's hair, tamed by water into retted jute, hangs across the ripe marble of her back, the shower steam follows her like a reluctant halo, and the cloying smell of honeysuckle soap, one of her vices, has washed the delicious acid perfume from her limbs. He turns his eyes to the fatal glare of the large metal vats where newspaper for collages curdles in paste and water, it is late, she says, and in her voice, a mild impatience swirls like a few faint bubbles, but he buries his face in the pillow, wishing he could stay, then wishing, suddenly, that he were alone, wishing to taste again of the forgotten mysteries of solitude, the sweet sound of his own breath uninterrupted by the rhythm of another life, the first sense of solitude had descended upon him when in his first year after college, the year when he taught

English to prissy little girls in a mediocre private school, he had been overcome by the beauty of being truly alone, in the two weeks that Trevor ran off to Spain with Catherine, and for the first time, one evening, the flat was replete with silence. Never had he experienced such heady silence, not in his home, with his mother drifting in dry shadows from room to room, the quiet rustle he had come to love, a silence full of death, a silence that was the absence of his sister's sandy laughter, the slap of her night cream upon her resilient skin, a heavy, musty silence. Even in his college room, sick with loneliness, he had felt uninsulated from the world without, the bawdy shrieks of men and women forced into an extended adolescence, in the crowded Union pool, he had sought silence, spreading himself upon the water, his ears submerged, eyes to the bright ceiling, until a blind and beautiful limb would thrash out upon his face, and he would pretend to drown, Phlebas the Phoenician, a fortnight dead.

She draws aside the heavy curtain to let in the night, it wanders uneasily through the ghostly suspensions of folded paper. And if this were to be the landscape of her mind? The longing grows dense to sculpt within herself the refuge of insanity, sweet madness, engulfing its own indignity between its blameless horizons. Yet, in this world, insanity has its own dignity, its own peace, in this land, insanity is like a pine forest, marching heedless into a blizzard, not the tropical insanity of wet, churned earth, the hyena shriek of the mad beggarwoman, searching in her spidery hair for invisible lice. If her mind were now to sprout a maze of stark conifers in which she might be permanently lost, wander from tree to tree, touching them as a woman might touch her lovers in the moments before execution? This remote beauty of madness had always been hidden from her, ruined in the coarse tropical sunshine, madness lurked like buried bloodstains, in the ugly oblivion of the retarded child in school playing tiddlywinks against his teeth, in the silent agony of the landlord's son, in his mezzanine prison, his brains beaten to pulp by police batons, long ago, they had watched him once, a forbidden pastime, she and her brother had taken turns, while he stood on the lookout she had peeped through the curtain in the landing window, he crouched, half-clothed, upon his bed, his hands spread out before him, she had never seen anyone sit so still, and then he turned his chalky eyes upon her, one of them hideously blind, she had let the curtain fall and swallowed the shriek that boiled up her throat. But it is not that unbecoming insanity that beckons to her now, it is the sharp geometry of bare conifers against white snow, the painful resolution of individual grass blades in a wide summer field, a forest of glass threads drained clean of desire, mute waves crashing without sound upon swollen sand.

Such a silence he had never known before, as that which nudged up against the nape of his neck, one evening, as he sat marking compositions, two days after he had come back from work to find a note stabbed against the wall, Trevor's tidy confession, love had fallen upon them out of the sky as he and Catherine had sat down to an afternoon breakfast, and to indulge in their newfound lust, and spare them all some embarrassment, for it was Anthony's bed that Catherine had warmed for the past few months, they had taken the first flight to Barcelona. Suffused with maturity, he had plucked the note from the flaking plaster, smiling quietly, he had stood in the doorway of Trevor's room, letting his eyes wander contentedly over the fragments of their shallow desire, and in his own room, he had allowed his toes to rub against the silk of Catherine's abandoned camisole, swelling under the duvet, reveling in the absence of desire, in the tender affection that he felt for them both. And when, in the evening, solitude had come to nest within the crook of his neck, he had found a far more skillful bedfellow than the sea-eyed girl who had just left him, the lips that had scattered cold pebbles upon his tongue. From then on, he and Trevor had shared their women, until, despite this, they had drifted gently apart, the lease ran out, Trevor moved in with four middle-aged Scandinavian sisters whom he had met at his yoga classes, it's like living in a Bergman film, he would say at parties, and Anthony, in pursuit of solitude, had squandered his meager income on an apartment to himself, Sunday luncheons he would take with Trevor in a house draped with cats, the gaunt sisters wiping fish threads from their furrowed underlips with lace napkins.

Her hair has dried now in thick creamy terraces, you really ought to leave, she says, he sits up and sifts through the clothes at his feet that she has gathered from the floor, what if I stay, he asks.

She shrugs, he struggles with heavy fisherman's knit, you too shall pass, he murmurs to himself in the meshes of strangulated wool.

And, later, as he moves cautiously past his daughter's door, his stockinged feet catch the edge of a fallen photograph, the river-bend of Anna's neck, meandering silver towards windmilled hair, will she, too, pass from his life, rise as ripe evening mist. In Burgundy, while they gazed speechless upon a lake of sunflow-ers, he had reached out boldly to grasp the burnished porcelain of her thigh, his knuckles had bled on the rough wall that she stood against, and his fingers had wandered breathless between the eggshell curves of her thighs, but he had not shared her with solitude, and yet when the daggerflowers in his flesh will have dissolved into pale foam, only solitude will remain. He lifts his tired eyes towards the glistening darkness above, Moni, you're not up there, still, are you, he asks, as if he has expected to return at two in the morning and find her rummaging in the

attic, she presses the wire brush hard against her scalp, he
staggers heavily into the room, what were you looking for, he
pulls his sweater over his neck, you could have waited, I would
have got it down, he hands her the sweater, she answers suddenly, the Scandinavian salad bowls, he yawns, I'm growing old,
he says, I'm so fearfully tired, she lifts the harsh wool to her
nostrils, there have never been any Scandinavian salad bowls,
are there such things as Scandinavian salad bowls, but she must
not court insanity through aggressive absurdity, although tonight, she has crossed the harsh boundaries of truth in her desire
to mesmerize, to hold their attention, she has told them of how
her flower pots came to be crushed under cruel police boots,
when it was not her story at all, but that of a friend, who had
woken one morning, as a child, to find the wild beds of white
rajanigandha flowers, flowers of the evening, by the stale pond,
trampled under sharp boots, her flower pots had been crushed
by the mischievous boy upstairs, whose brother, it was true, was
soon to be taken away by the police, but he had returned, alive,
porridge-brained, and he had never given her toffee eclairs,
even in sanity, when he stalked arrogantly in to lend books to her
brother, even before they took him away, he had been terrify-
ingly aloof, it was the Marwari businessman's son from the large
house next door with checkered parapets that brought her toffee
eclairs, in broken Bengali he would amuse their mother, dark
eyes darting in a mashed-potato complexion, afraid, somehow, it
seemed, of the enormous gobs of time on his hands, ponderous
afternoon hours, but her father had not approved of his intru-
sion, and when, during her mother's appendectomy, he had
proved indispensable with his car, constantly at their service,
her father had accepted his kindness with a gratitude stiff as
coconut wire, when the boy's father had ordered him to Bombay
to oversee the diversification of their business into bone ash and
glue, their mother had been overcome by a depthless depression

that she had never been able to comprehend, and, of course, the stream of toffee eclairs had been stymied, leaving only a few minor dental casualties, that glinted still in the weak morning light in the broad bathroom mirror, she hangs his trousers over a chair, he eases gratefully between the sheets, I'm so bloody tired, he says, it's unbelievable.

The Scandinavian sisters, smelling of wet matchsticks, and Trevor, vowed to celibacy, reading to them from the Upanishads on Sunday afternoons, the soft sucking sounds of their knitting needles, wrestling with thick boiled wool, Anthony would lie back against brocade cushions, a few Persian cats, and the grain husks that drifted down from the canary cage in the window, they sent their painful woolen creations to a missionary cousin in Calcutta, but surely it is too hot there, he had asked, for such heavy garments, and they had told him, with deep pity in their voices for his ignorance, that from their cousin, the clothes went to North Bengal and Bihar, the damp Himalayan foothills, that summer he came, the portly padre, peeling tropical scabs, and lo and behold, it appeared that his long association with Calcutta was cultural as well as spiritual, insofar as they are distinct, Trevor hastened to add, his foam-flecked image in the bathroom mirror swaying dangerously as Anthony opened the cabinet, what is that you are taking, firewater, camphor and honey, deep treacle, apothecary's delight, it's for my throat, want some, it's delicious, in those days, while the dream of becoming an actor still clung like slow seaweed he took great pains to maintain his voice, a possible asset, a reluctant agent had told him once, he replaces the bottle and shuts the door, the tube of shaving cream has crawled into the tub, this Father, Trevor continued, runs a small film institute, it would seem, within the confines of his ecclesiastical duties, it's quite remarkable, the razor cuts clean into the moldy lather on Anthony's chin, where did you get that medieval instrument, Trevor asks, Portobello Road, he mumbles through the bubbles, it's quite remarkable, says Trevor, surreal even, they have diploma courses and a large library, his favorite film, of course, is Pasolini's *Gospel,* and lather creases in laughter upon Anthony's cheeks, but there is hesitation in Trevor's mirth, he was quite articulate about it, actually, he says, at dinner last night. I'm meeting him for lunch, he says, ignoring Anthony's quizzical look, we're meeting at St. Martin's-in-the-Fields, want to come? By the time they arrived, the Father was waiting, sweating under his burden of book bags, in the dim crypt he laid out his purchases for them to see, several dog-eared secondhand screenplays—for our film library, he explained proudly.

Many years later, when Moni, while composing her application to the local library, had asked him if she should mention under Previous Experience the summer of '76 when she had been assistant to Gayatri at the Institute Library, only then had it hit him, with all the cheap glory of coincidence, that it would have been the same time as when the Father was running his loving hands across the creased paperbacks in the gloom of the Café in the Crypt of St. Martin's-in-the-Fields, thinking perhaps of how she might help him unpack them later, make space for them upon the dusty shelves, sweet Moni, favorite among the Father's many favorites, it was he who had suggested that she spend the summer working for the Institute, the summer of '76, that glorious gap between school and college, awaiting her examination results, she had taken the tram every morning to the old church, Gayatri was always late, and she would knock, timidly, at the Father's office for the keys, he greeted her with great affection, always, the Father who had never been a father, and in relinquishing fatherhood had come to father them all, those gnarled fingers had never touched a woman, and yet he lectured with ease on sexuality and cinema. For this her brother and his friends laughed at him, even gracious Gayatri, who paid her mother's hospital bills from her income as custodian of the odd collection of books and journals that they called the library, their callous mirth offended her, a blind ball of hurt that she gulped amid their laughter, for she had found great peace in the dry afternoons, dusting copies of *Sight and Sound* by the tall tree-fingered windows, and then there were afternoons when there was simply nothing to do but sit behind the issue desk and read until someone came in to whisper that warm samosas were being circulated in the seminar room, and she and Gayatri would make trips in turn, and then the satisfying drip of the melting afternoon once again, the rustle of dignified paper, and languid church bells, measuring out the lacustrine hours.

At ten minutes to five, she would get up to gently tap the last few readers on their shoulders, the old film critic who came in to catch a few minutes of sleep every day, around four, when he tired of the energetic conversation around him, he had given up reading long ago, one last loving look around the room, the tall heavy doors hauled shut, by then, often, they would have gathered, her brother, and the rest of them, or if it was an early film that evening, she and Gayatri would meet them at the hall, and then there were afternoons when she would fight her way back home alone, through the crosscurrents of humanity, to abandon herself to the unshackled evening hours, it had been a happy summer.

The Father presented Anthony with a copy of Tagore's *Red Oleanders*, originally intended for one of his spinster cousins, but the Scandinavian sisters appeared not to care much for plays, the Father told him sadly, and the cinema, of course, is to them an utterly alien phenomenon!

Did Tagore make any films at all? asked Anthony, flicking through the slim volume, for he had learned from the Father that the poet was much more than a poet: playwright, novelist, essayist, musician, and in old age, a fearless painter, did he never explore the medium of cinema? Anthony asked.

He appreciated cinema, the Father replied, of that there is evidence: he even said that for cinema to establish itself as an independent art form, it must sever its umbilical with literature, very progressive, don't you think, said the Father, shaking an early autumn leaf off his shoe, very progressive for a man of his time.

Yet, to Moni, there was something faintly obscene about the idea that the poet had seen *Battleship Potemkin,* a rude clash of images within her when Gayatri mentioned triumphantly that he had even sent his congratulations to Eisenstein, she cannot see him, even now, stroking his luxuriant beard in the dark of a cinema hall, or worse still, if he were to have experimented with the art, to be squinting into the eye of a camera, his robes trailing studio sawdust, he, whom she had thought, for the greater part of her childhood, to be one of the gods, if only for the curious coincidence by which Tagore, or Thakur as is its unbastardized form, means Lord in Bengali, the Lord Krishna, Krishna Thakur, and Rabindranath Thakur, the Lord Rabindranath, perched upon soft cloud, heavenly poet, floating his verse upon wind-stream, to fall as rich rain upon earth, and when she had discovered, in shame and disbelief, that he had only been a man, had died, like all men, only eighteen years before her birth, she recognized then that a mortal may command more reverence than the gods themselves, and it was then that she swore to him, perhaps, in the words that he had given her,

> if the doors to my heart should someday close upon you
> break them down and enter my soul
> remember you are my only king, do not turn away.

Exciting things are happening in theater, the Father told him, upon the grassy banks of the Serpentine, our librarian is associated with a group of young people who put on rather alarm-ingly experimental plays, they have become very popular, a wonderful group, such intelligent young people, and so enthusiastic about life, it's what I like to see, you know, an old man like me, that life has meaning for the young, life is so very precious, and it had seemed to him, suddenly, that perhaps the answers to all his questions about life and art lay concealed in the mired metropolis of whom the Father spoke with such dense affection, that the edges of claustrophobic blue that had begun to curl about the corners of his existence might be washed clean by hard tropical perspiration, and also that it was an eminently fundable project that the cleric was laying out before him, he telephoned his mother that night, I am thinking of going to India, he told her, for my research, and she had sighed and said, my uncle is buried in India, perhaps you can visit his grave.

The rains came late, that summer, after the Father had left for England, one afternoon, dark clouds began to gather, grim warriors before battle, churning wet gunpowder from the parched blue, the trees sighed, and she ran with beating heart to draw in the large shutters, and not fast enough, dusty slivers of new rain sank into the pile of little magazines that someone had left on the sill, and with the windows shut, the dim lights that dangled from the high ceiling came on, and the library took on an unfamiliar air of gloom. She sat despondently, hoping to immerse herself in the sounds of thunder, closing her eyes to shut out the pasty light, humming rain tunes to herself until Gayatri told her, a little impatiently, that the readers might find this distracting, so when the storm was over, she rushed to throw open the shutters, let in the convalescent air, weak but pure from battle, and the smell of hibiscus crushed in new mud, but the new brightness was unbearably shallow, devoid of the subharmonic layers of light that the dry sun had wrought between the shelves, from the pavement below came the flap of wet tarpaulin over the tea stalls, things would never be the same again.

* * *

It took two years for him to gather funds, convince his professors, placate his girlfriend—a wasted effort, for, in any case, in the week before he left, they parted stormily—two summers later, brimming with hope, he found himself walking gingerly across the burning tarmac to International Arrivals, the Father waving excitedly from the gallery, he spent a week in the sparse room at the Mission before moving to the marbled comfort of Amrita's mansion, the Father had been hurt, naturally. It is a better way to become acquainted with the culture, surely, Anthony had offered by way of explanation, and the Father had nodded silently.

Indeed, he had given the old padre very little of his time, immersed as he was in the pursuit of the sublime, and yet, one morning, soon after they had decided to marry, he insisted that they visit him together, for a blessing? she had asked incredulously, no, of course not, but he had grown tired, in the past few days, of the solemn smiles that greeted his announcement of their engagement, the sad stiff handshakes, the awkward celebratory meal at the Moulin Rouge, he had begun to attribute this despondence not to the peculiarity of their circumstances but to some facet of the culture, in which marriage was perhaps merely an inevitability, as he drew her reluctantly in through the church gates, he cherished the hope that the Father would grasp his hand in a gesture of simple goodwill, that no one else had offered until now, that it was wrong of him to demand from a culture where the union of man and woman was perhaps regarded as too personal, too delicate to be shared among others except in prolonged ritual, elaborate institutional revelry, and during the wedding as he sat, his hand bound in hers, insulated by thick smoke from the raucous celebration, it had struck him, once again, we are not part of this, we have been cleaved, scooped out, the thin wooden door that rattled between them and the vast troop of guests who sang and joked late into the night had seemed an impenetrable barrier as his frenzied fingers traveled among the sharp gold threads of her garment, drawing apart the moist petrifaction of her flesh, he had penetrated into the heart of a deep tropical silence.

Perhaps the Father will help her now, prodigal daughter, she will unload herself to him, tell him that her only salvation now is in the succor of human woe, that she will serve him now, not as she did before, dusting magazines and reshelving, but by tending the sick, the poor, the Father will know where she must go, what there is to be done, after all, it was he who had told her brother, much to his amusement but more to his delight, there is something angelic about your sister, she reminds one of the Holy Virgin, who was after all, he had added, dark like her, it had been a wonderful summer, the summer of '76.

It was the same feeling then, that crams its fingers up her now, as it was on that day that her brother rushed like a mad wind into the library brandishing a scrap of paper, her examination results, the gazettes are out, he shouted, and you, his voice sank to an emotional whisper, you have done wonderfully well, and it had seemed to her suddenly that she was finally upon the shores of a quiet ocean, and the sea smell had returned to her again, two years later, in the Chinese restaurant on Free School Street as she submitted to the fantasy of marriage, and in these last few hours, the winds return, tempered now with the smell of decayed seaweed, for she has seen the sea now, stood upon the crumbling chalk shores, chalk fingers rising defiantly from the dull waters, old Harry and his wife, breeding cormorants, she has choked back the desire to leap across the splintered chasms, like the restless birds, she looks around at him, suddenly awake, locked in his own memories, a slow smile spreading over his tired cheeks, she longs to tell him, there is a wind, a great wet wind, in my heart.

He lies back against the pillows and contemplates the harmony of his existence, it is a time of success, a time to live, for himself, for his friends, life has finally begun, after years of bitter struggle, of dense despair, of discovery and deceit, a limpid strength imbues his being, the attic door shuts suddenly upon his thoughts, she drags the chair into the room, he is immersed in a satisfying gratitude, she has seen him through it all, she has come back after long hours at the Public Library, smelling of dead ink, her fingers bruised with books, her calves sore from standing for hours, mindlessly issuing books, while he has fretted and banged upon his typewriter, she has cleared away the debris of his frustrations without a murmur, cooked him dinner, she has borne him his child, his angel, she has spent many lonely evenings while he has drowned the forgotten poetry of his soul in the ivory billows of another woman's flesh, but everything he has done is for the both of them, this he longs to tell her, to wipe the mute anguish from her eyes, all will pass from our lives, he longs to say, but you for me and me for you, he sees them, old and withered, looking back, contented, upon the expanse of their lives, he feels today, that many more women will have come and gone, and someday after he is dust, she will sit down to write of him and his loves, of their life together, and her black eyes will cloud with the beauty of pain, as they had done, many years ago, when he had first whispered to her of their fruitless love. But the purity of that emotion had been, in some sense, regressive, it had muted his creativity, she must respect that, he had loved her with a force that had drowned his powers of analysis, the last years had been a struggle to regain that sublime balance between emotion and intellect, and yet he had felt nothing so painful as the passing of his passion, he had hoped, in the damp darkness of a tropical winter, that he might be able to live on love alone.

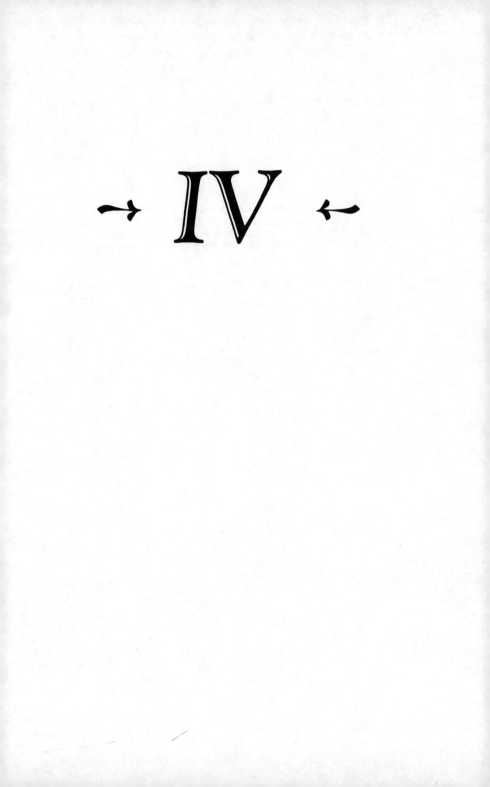

VI

Worn velvet dark, night merges into day, between cold thimblefuls of sleep she sees their life pass before her eyes, in high summer she had spread her hair upon the banks of the Thames and thought, if she should die now, the grass warm upon her neck, she would not have the energy to let her life flash by, in the protracted second before her death, her blood would lap lazily against her veins instead of coursing back through time within her terrified mind, and now the story of their love unwinds rapidly within her, in that painfully lucid moment before sleep, and when she finally wakes, a bright sunlight streams through the crack in the curtains, it is ten in the morning, he has left, she will never see him again, so this was the dissatisfaction of death, the incomplete symmetry, she had thought long into the darkness of how she might kiss him goodbye, instead she has slept through the last hours of their life together, her last memory of him will not be his broad unsuspecting smile through the car window, she sits up suddenly, ten o'clock, he must have taken the child to school, her blood runs cold at the thought of retrieving her, she had meant to keep her at home, no school for you today, he has gone, the fragile remains of the morning hang upon her fingers, still lacquered in sleep, he has gone leaving a shadow of his lips, that might indeed have been dream, this last irony of his absence, robbing her of the poetry of farewell, scattering far the skeins of her desire that she had hoped to tie into one cruel knot with her last wave, and yet, if she is to go, there is no longer any time to muse, to regret, she clothes herself hastily, she must collect the tickets, the birthday cake, she washes the blood-specked foam off the toothbrush, no time for a cup of tea, she grabs her handbag, the front door shuts with a resolute bang, the sky welcomes her with a sharp blueness, she picks her way steadily through the obstacle course of dog feces, London pavements, towards the Tube station, the trees lift their ragged branches to the clear cold sky, dripping dead leaves that swirl like sodden cornflakes about her feet, she runs across the High Street, she must not panic, she tells herself, she rushes down the littered stairs, the train doors close upon her as she arrives, but then, for some inscrutable reason, they slide open again, she enters gratefully, a bee is trapped between the two panes in the window, how did it ever get there, the woman beside her is reading a magazine article called "Getting Rid of Rodney"—why were all the nicest girls mad, married, or murderesses—she reads, the woman senses her eyes upon the page and closes it abruptly, the English were so possessive of their tabloids, she scrutinizes the advertisements, her eyes fall with delight upon a slice of poetry, Poems on the Underground, between Handsome Hints 3 from Corby of Windsor, and the angelic countenance of a girl advertising face masks, wide innocent eyes edged with a nourishing slime, as a young girl she had used sandalwood paste, cucumber juice, coarse flour in thick curd, her mother would rub milk-skin upon her arms until it rolled off stiff with dirt, she squints to read the poem, Keats, Keats again, an appropriate requiem, it is not a favorite poem though, "On First Looking into Chapman's Homer," *Much have I travelled in the realms of gold,* the words echo within her in the weedy voice of the temporary lecturer who had taught them Romantic Poetry for two painful summer months, will she never be rid of the ghost of her dispassionate tones, grinding out the lusty syllables into the humid air, they had given her a very difficult time, how vicious they had been in their youthful exuberance, they had drawn tears from her dull bloodshot eyes, as they mimicked her terrible pronunciation, *Maach heb I trebhelled in the realms oph gold*, they had giggled behind clenched fists while the boldest of them stood and read, and the teacher's thick glasses had misted over with tears, who knows where she was now, she had hidden her face in shame once as she caught sight of her upon a local train, she must have made a long journey every day to come and teach them, the carefree, insolent city girls, and her mother must have been so proud, her daughter, too unattractive to marry off without a large dowry, while her friends had borne children, she had studied into the night for a Ph.D. in English, the language of the lords, a job at one of the best Calcutta colleges, be it temporary, and the money would pay for her brother's schoolbooks, or perhaps she had spurned the idea of marriage herself, choosing instead the bitter freedom of her books, or perhaps like her aunt she had run from her husband's home, the bed of torture, some of the girls suggested, jokingly, she might be married to a progressive Marxist who forbade vermilion in her parting, but she had recognized upon those charred, emaciated limbs the absence of a man's touch, in the wooden anguish of her voice, droning on, *He stared at the Pacific—and all his men, Look'd at each other with a wild surmise—Silent, upon a peak in Darien,* the train jerks to a sudden halt, Warren Street, she rushes off, the escalators are not working, her head swims at the optical rhapsody of the numerous steel lines upon the escalator steps as she climbs quickly to the top, Tottenham Court Road, here she had walked alone, for the first time, in London, the first day at the damp flat near Turnpike Lane, after a week in Bristol with his mother, he had asked her to meet him at Dillons, given her instructions on how to get there, and so for the first time she had walked through the streets of London alone, and it had filled her with a sense of profound wonder, that she should be alone with this great city, her toes cramped within the shiny new boots that his mother had bought her, the unfamiliar roughness of nylon chafing at her thighs, she had walked upon the very streets that Dickens, Hardy, Virginia Woolf had trod, and today is her last day among these vast spirits, she has not read any serious literature since she set foot upon this land, perhaps she will rediscover them, in the still shadows of a tropical afternoon, while the child sleeps beside her, perhaps, once again, she will immerse herself in thick suet-colored leaves of a ragged volume, the passions of a past whose reek she had inhaled, newsprint soaked in fish oil, the diseased saliva of underground rodents, the graceless vocabulary of a new arrogance, at the travel agent's the magenta lips of a pale subcontinental girl close upon a chewed pen as she rummages through her card file, she watches the leaky ballpoint move upon the thin strips of paper, her passport to a different dream, and it is far too unreal to be of comfort, as indeed it had been, on a winter morning, ten years ago, at the British Airways office in Chowringee, she sat fingering her virgin passport, and watched a withered hand fill hieroglyphics upon the carbon sheets, the man wore a shirt patterned with small bicycles, this obscure detail rubs sharp among unwanted memories, it is far too bright outside, the fierce blue burns through the shop glass, but she has rehearsed this, over and over, last night, in soiled sunlight, she has detailed the meager shadows upon her trembling fingers as she picks up the ticket, and instead the flat fluorescence wavers coldly upon her stiff hands, she murmurs, thank you, and instead of rising from her seat, she lingers, her eyes frozen upon the girl, in her dreams, there had been a harsh mountain, sprouting orchids, where the girl gapes restless magenta, in her dreams she had pushed open the funereal door to the travel agent's offices and come face to face with a mountain, and before this dream, there was another, where grave sympathetic eyes had gazed from the shadows in quiet understanding, in deep assent, and out upon the street, he had passed with his lover, for he worked nearby, and they had stopped in horror, that story ended there, frozen upon her petrified eyes, and their faces, blanched with disbelief outside the murky glass, but other fantasies came, fast and thick, it will be Trevor perhaps who will halt outside the window, squinting in the shadows, and walking down Tottenham Court Road, she will unburden herself to him, and in the end, it is he who will drive them to the airport, and to Anthony, sitting in the dark, after the party, his head in his hands, he will say, she has left you, as indeed she should have done, long ago, Trevor, who had said, so often, in lead-lined jocosity, you should just leave the bastard, the girl twirls her pen impatiently, a door bursts open, and music streams suddenly into the sunlit room, *last night I slept in sheets the color of fire*, she starts, apologizes and stands up, and yet, once again, at the door she halts, turns to look back, is there to be nothing more to this treasured exercise, no awkward questions, will her dark sorrow not thicken the air in dignified gloom, will she pass unnoticed from the lives of these people, purveyors of freedom, lost in the sunshine stream of customers, they will not mark this day with the memory of issuing her a ticket, for it is, after all, an ordinary day in the lives of most people, the last bright day of the year, and yet there are people who will die today and be born, bereaved, ruined, corrupted, transfigured, with them she feels a fruitless kinship, the door slams behind her, too loud, she is out again in the glare of the street, she walks across the road, over to Gower Street, past the Accident and Emergency Ward of University College Hospital, here she had visited Trevor, every afternoon, three years ago, when he had tried to slit his wrists, she had sat at his side in the grim ward, held his bandaged hands as he cried, she had not been capable of compassion then, but he had found comfort in her blank eyes, he had found her silence more diverting than the careful conversation of the flock of friends that would descend upon him in the evenings, so he had told her, spilling cold tears, bloodless eyelids, and she had seen him yesterday, flushed with success, her last memory of him would be the childlike confidence of his bright eyes hovering over a sea of champagne glasses, she waits for a bus to take her to the patisserie, she must collect the cake, troughs of cold icing will lie stiff in the empty air, the empty stairs echoing the unsteady footfalls of a child that has left forever, the sour steam of old milk stains, the bus arrives, she climbs to the upper deck and sits down gingerly beside an overweight woman in a pastel sweatsuit, clouds race in the clear sky, the movements of the crowd upon the pavement are outlined in glass, the cold fragrance of condensed sugar settles around her as she enters the shop, the licorice tendrils of a black, spider-shaped pudding rub against the syrup-stained glass, the cake is altogether too lifelike, a squat bunny with a toffee nose, it is difficult to believe that under the shag of white icing, raisins and candied peel conspire with dark sponge, one ear droops delicately over a translucent red eye, can you eat the eyes, she asks, yes, they too are one of the many guises of sugar, like blown glass, she is moved by a strange wistfulness in their carmine depths, she has always been sensitive to the proud despair of all that is edible, sleek aubergines slaughtered mercilessly under steel knives, cauliflower heads bowing bitterly to their fate, but she feels immense relief that she will not have to slice through the white sugar paws, hold out the red eyes for little mouths to suck, the cake is heavy in her hands, she takes a taxi home.

She sets the cake box upon the kitchen counter and licks the encrustations of sugar off her fingers, she glances worriedly at her watch, she must fetch the child from school, there is no time to lose, she rushes out again into the bright sunlight, through the park, dragging dead leaves, over the hill, the school comes into view, a dull glare comes from within the tarmac of the play-ground, she pushes open the rusty gate, a smell of boiled lamb wafts down the corridor, she walks quickly up the stairs to the child's classroom, the children are lined up against the window with their backs to her, a plump young woman leans over their shoulders, she knocks and as the woman lifts her head she moves through the maze of desks towards her, trays of wet cotton wool line the long sill, they are growing watercress, the child looks up and smiles, she wears a cardboard placard upon her pullover proclaiming that she is six today, she giggles and whispers to her friends, but the teacher looks worried, she does not have the authority to let her leave, she explains, they must see the head-mistress, she takes them downstairs and shows them into a small room, would you wait here please, and she is gone, she pulls the child onto her lap, she remembers, many years ago, she had waited in the hallway outside the Mother Superior's office at her college, the hallway hung with paintings of the Raj, of the good Queen Victoria, and finally the forbidding doors had opened, and drawing her shawl about her she had entered the sparse office to explain that she was leaving for that very land whose language she had come to learn within the halls of this hallowed institution, and the Mother had held her hand and asked her to promise that she would not ever relinquish the pursuit of knowl-edge, God has laid at your feet a unique opportunity, she had said, you must not disappoint him, and the following year, when she had decided to send her a Christmas card, she had chewed on her pen and wondered how she could tell her that she was working at a library, certainly that news had brought many tearful letters from her mother, how could she have known she was sending her child into poverty and disgrace, she had read them chalk-faced behind her morning cup of tea, thanking the heavens that Anthony could not read the language, and yet that was, without doubt, the happiest time of her life, the first deluge of homesickness had disappeared leaving the comforting damp of unripe nostalgia, their love had reached a state of secure peace, quiet evenings when he would read to her, she might try falteringly to translate a song until she would shake her head despairingly and bury it upon his chest, her thoughts are interrupted by the solid click of hard heels outside, the headmistress, instinctively, she lets the child slip down and raises herself from the armchair, the woman motions her to sit, and takes a chair across from her, now, what is the matter, she asks anxiously, locking her hands in front of her knees, she needs an explanation, but there is none, nothing comes to her mind, dry with fear, she sits mute, I really cannot explain, she says, the headmistress' eyes harden, in this country, we take schooling very seriously, she says, she cannot let the child go home unless there is a very good reason for her to do so, Moni bites her lip, surely it is her right, but she cannot find the words to say so, there is a knock upon the door, a young girl, probably her secretary, announces an important telephone call, if you will excuse me for a few minutes, the footsteps die away outside, suddenly it is clear what she must do, she rises quickly from her chair, lifts the child into her arms, and walks out through the door, down the corridor, onto the slippery tar, the schoolbell rings, children begin to spill out of the classrooms, she steps over the low wall, walks rapidly up the hill, a black taxi is lumbering down, she seizes it, she asks the driver to wait outside the house, she seats the child in the dining room, quickly pours her a glass of milk, she calls the driver in to help with the suitcases, in the kitchen, she fills a plastic container with sandwiches, destroying the symmetry of a plate she has arranged with deliberate care, last night, while they hung decorations, this is her last glimpse of the kitchen, in the dining room, she gazes wistfully upon the table that she was to have decorated with food, but somehow she is glad she has not succumbed to that petty irony, a glass gondola sits upon the sideboard, she had insisted on its purchase, many years ago, in Murano, and he had despised it, she stuffs it hastily into her handbag, come on, she says to the child, where are we going, the girl asks meekly, somewhere very nice, she says, lifting her into the taxi, somewhere far away, what about her party, her eyebrows arch in an unfamiliar expression of confused defiance, what about my party, her small palms press in futile aggression against the cab window, and within Moni, a wall of glass crumbles under the weight of depthless remorse, and yet an acid cruelty tingles pleasurably against her palate, her cheek against the child's tearstained flesh, she watches the potted plants lift their weak faces away from her, there under the hyssop we planted your first tooth, this summer, for weeks you would run eagerly outside to see if it had sprouted, Anthony found this morbid, and steadying the child's hand with her little red water can, she had reminded him, her eyes buried in blue whorls of hyssop flower, she had reminded him that it was Anna who, upon hearing that they had buried the tooth, had convinced the child it would burgeon into a tooth-tree, for proof she had brought for her, the next day, a pomegranate, whose seeds, little teeth, buried in sweet gum flesh, were what she might find, one bright morning, among the hyssop, it was Anna who had let her imagination run wild, confessing to Moni, in the kitchen, that this might be some delayed revenge against the shadowed figure in her childhood who had warned her that apple seeds, when swallowed, burst into bloom within the caverns of one's body, snaking up the gullet, and bursting through the nostrils to dangle sweet apples in front of one's mouth, how we love to torture our children, she had thought then, silently wiping the dishes, while Anna, laughing, went on to describe how, terrified that her insides would turn to bark, she had nevertheless been exhilarated by the discovery, in a schoolbook of her sister's, of a man afflicted by such a fate, his skin, it seemed, had been cut away to reveal the meanderings of the treacherous twigs within his chest, but of course, Anna said, a little wistfully, it was only a sketch of a pair of very normal lungs, it was Anna, she told Anthony, her face stinging with hyssop, who put such ideas into her head, for she had helped her bury it, as her grandmother had, many years ago, in the stony patch of land beside the veranda of their Ballygunge home, for rats to carry away, and with the rats' blessing, sharp rodent teeth would sprout upon your tiny gum, her grandmother had explained, touching the tender gap between her teeth with a horny finger, they had knelt by the stairs to the veranda, scratching in the hard soil, and years later, when the area was cemented over, playing a miniature hopscotch, she would think of her many teeth that lay trapped under the hard cement, had the rats ever found them?

In thin streaks of tired green, the plants slip away, the balm and the bay, camomile, comfrey and cornflower, optimistic euca-lyptus, marigolds, flowers of damp death, and parsley, marsh-mallow and mullein, and in the hollows by the doorway, forests of mint, that fumbling with his keys after a night of dense adul-tery, he might hone his satisfied desire on its sharp perfume, and perhaps today, he will search in quiet disbelief for the pungent stains of mint leaf, crushed under many impatient little feet, voices that do not rise to meet him as he hammers upon the door, or perhaps they will be waiting, confused faces scrubbed healthy raw, tapping their neat shoes upon the flagstones, twisting thyme stalk, perhaps, choking back his anger, for it will be anger at first that will flood his complacent being, restraining the bitter bubbles of wrath that are beginning to stream into his mouth, he will open the doors, the front door, hastily shut, not double-locked, a sign that they might not be far away, and then the inner door, wreathed in crude frosted glass, the keys still dan-gling from the keyhole, his fingers will close around the mystery of their presence, she can feel the jagged cold of key-metal biting into his fingers, those hands, that she had feared, once, might bruise themselves upon the ice-cold shards of her wintry hair, she hopes will bleed upon the shock of her abandoned keys, she twists around in the taxi for a last glimpse of the red gate they had painted together, he and the child, red nails that she had scrubbed until she screamed, and flecks of shining red fell disturbingly like petrified blood onto the pale porcelain.

The child is stiff in her arms, as she raises a sandwich to her lips, her face still turned to the window, the lips resist briefly, then, as if mechanically, close around the sandwich, where are we going, she asks again, what about my party?

You will have your party, she tells her, in a voice, unbearably calm, like a river of sugar, and it seems to her that the child winces, you will have your party, she says, a little sternly, she remembers, hopping through the strands of broken light from the ventilators, in the corridor outside the kitchen, a summer afternoon, the smell of boiled birthday sweets, a cake that her aunt from Canada has managed to bake, somehow, in a pan, her grandmother tugs at her hair, time for a bath, an order reluctantly obeyed, although the cold water from the deep water drum falls pleasantly icy upon her nape, and the abrasive thin towel, a price for the pleasure to come, for as the shadows in the corridor begin to fade, the neighbors will arrive, with presents wrapped in thin marbled paper that fell apart so easily in her hands, and yet the aggressive string refused to yield, the presents remained incongruously trussed, until her brother, masking his own excitement with an air of supreme indifference, came forward to lend a hand, and then the bindings would release their wares, for it was books mainly that they gave her, from classic children's stories, piled high in duplicates to be recirculated, despite her great reluctance, at other inconsequential birthdays, to garish modern fiction, stories of kidnapped children, maimed and sent out to beg in the streets, a blind boy who

calls after his mother, it is I, it is your very own son, did the
mother turn away in horror and disbelief, or take him home to
spend the rest of his days in comfort, and blindness, she cannot
remember, but how could such a story have ended well, as a
child's story should, for it is only their private hell that we
ignore, unfinished stories of monsters and dragons that will be
with them forever, of appleseeds drawing sustenance from the
lining of your stomach and sending out cruel branches through
your body, which you must believe then to be solid, inviolable,
not hollow, as you might learn later to your disbelief, as indeed,
was the entirety of the physical world, her cousin had told her
excitedly, one evening as they sat studying for their secondary
examinations, this surface of wood, your desk, that responds so
rigidly to your touch, and buoys your textbooks so effortlessly, is
hollow, Moni, dreadfully hollow, speckled only with the sparse
dust of atomic nuclei and their insignificant satellites, whose
forces, it would seem, were enough to erect an impenetrable
barrier, between herself and the world beyond, these particles
that conspired to scatter light to belie their hollowness with
whorls and pitted troughs, all that she knew and loved to be
wood, and so we lade our children with unfinished tales, she
thought, a peep at the silent landscape of our adult realities, and
those tales that we feel compelled to end, we end happily, or at
least, in what we comprehend to be happiness, for the pleasure
of absurdity is an adult pleasure, she remembers many nights of
discomfort at the thought of monsters dismembered conve-
niently by plucking the wings off a bee, buried in a cask under
a deep, deep lake, of birds condemned to blindness unless their
eyes be anointed by drops of princely blood, the unfortunate
author who had embarked upon the story of the blind, beggar
child could call upon no such device, however, to rescue his
story, for he had undertaken to present the truth, as he knew the
truth to be, the very gruesome truth of institutionalized beggary,

but one which sat no less comfortably within a child than the strange truth in myth, heavy with inscrutable metaphor, the books had sold very well, even with a garish cover of the child's eyes streaming with blood, mother, it is I, your very own son, many years later, she dreamt of encountering a faceless lover, reduced to rags, in a strange unfamiliar land, possibly after a total apocalypse, and later as she fed upon her dream, she had garnished it with cinematic detail, her eyes traveling from a dirty hand tugging at her clothes to familiar eyes in a broken hungry face, is it you then, is it truly you, perhaps the fabric of this fantasy had derived from that wretched book, suddenly she remembers why the ending is so unclear, for one rainy afternoon, as she sat reading it, her eyes streaming with tears, her brother had seized it from her hands, you shouldn't be reading this junk, he had proclaimed, angry, with new authority, another unfinished story, you will have your party, she tells the child, her voice dissolving in tears, you will have your party, and there will be lots of new friends and cousins.

Don't want new friends, says the child, kicking her feet. She has always resisted change, she thinks, always suspicious of strangers, reluctant to accept new toys to her menagerie, she has drawn a circle about herself, child of a riven marriage, so utterly content, however, within her own boundaries, like her father, she cannot endure any disturbance in the scheme of things, we are going to travel, she tells the girl, to a new land, how those words had filled her with joy, as a child, a new land, unfamiliar trees, hills that do not know your name, wanderlust, I know not where the wide road runs, nor what the blue hills are, but the road calls, and the hills call, and oh, the call of a star, wanderlust, the curse of their race, you will see Big Ben, her brother had told her, in wistful despair on the night before she left, you will walk upon the chalk cliffs of Shakespeare's demi-paradise, you will inhale the winds of Wessex, you, not I, although they had driven

to Dorset, one weekend, last year, with him, and in their B&B,
Anthony shifted restlessly in bed, plagued, it seemed to her, by
the incongruous fear that next door, Anna might be submitting
to the caresses of her inebriated brother, for she had found him
delightfully amusing, and they had both been very comfortable
in each other's company in the pub, stopping in the graveyard
afterwards to take in Corfe Castle by the last rays of the sun, and
Anthony had stood by her side, irritatedly sober, while they
laughed and laughed, and talked of Dürrenmatt, and later as
they lay together with their child, they had heard their laughter
again, in the corridor, indistinct goodnights, and he had not been
able to barge out, as he surely would have done if their room had
not come with an attached bath, and so all night, he tossed and
turned, and all of Sunday wore the look of a haggard wounded
lover that must have endeared itself deeply to Anna, for when
he dropped her off later that night, he did not return until after
midnight, and still her brother turned a blind eye to her predicament, dozing in front of the television, sleepless herself, from
upstairs she heard Anthony shake him awake, for God's sake, go
to bed if you can't keep awake. We are going to a new country,
where your uncle lives, she tells the child, and in every new
country, there are new friends, lovely new friends, it's great fun
really going somewhere new, there's so much to see, so many
new people to love, so much to learn, her voice fades, she
remembers the one postcard the young American sent them,
many months after he had walked out of their front door without
farewell, he sent from South America a postcard with a very
explicit ethnic carving, a man with an enormous erection, and on
the back he had written, simply: the more you travel, the less
you know—Taoist saying, and while she breathed a sigh of relief
that it was not some embarrassing declaration of love, Anthony
had said with untold disgust, bloody ingrate, not a word of
thanks for all we did, these bloody Americans, and today, coax-

ing the lips of her child with another sandwich, she wonders if it would not have been more satisfying if he had declared his undying love for her on the back of a postcard, it would have to be a postcard, for Anthony would never have opened a letter to her, but no, it would have become an enormous joke, your American boyfriend, he would have dubbed him, but even so, perhaps, there might have been a hint of distress in his voice, his territory encroached upon, perhaps.

Near the Everyman Cinema, her hands begin, suddenly, to shake uncontrollably, she hides them behind her back, frightened and at the same time exhilarated by this rare loss of control, she turns her head to glance briefly up the narrow street where they had emerged cramped, many years ago, in her first week in England, after a Fellini triple bill, she had read in his face the distress that although she had been so eager to see the films, stoically borne the February cold through six stiff hours, having seen them, she had not much to say, and even so, as she nodded silently in answer to his question, did you enjoy that? did you? he had wrapped a long arm around her, around the licorice cascade of hair that she had released from a knot to warm her frozen shoulders, wear your hair like this, he had told her, wear it loose, my love, *And her hair is a long-lost night of the ancient kingdom of Bidisha,* an untranslatable line from a beloved poem by Jibanananda Das echoed within her, as he groped in hidden frenzy within the depths of her tresses. The streets of Hampstead race by, behind her, her hands begin to calm, even petrify, she draws them out stiffly, and takes another sandwich from the box on her lap and offers it to the child.

I'm not hungry, says the girl sullenly, and what about my cake?

This is merely my first inquisition, she reminds herself, in time she will not remember the cake, or the little girls that she called her friends, but she will ask, in the years to come, of her father, whom she will remember in windy scraps, which she will weld, according to her temperament, into an ideal of love or images of rejection, and she will ask, why was it that one bright autumn afternoon she was torn from her cocoon of peace with such unnecessary violence, what grand whim of her mother's was this, of which she might be the victim. And yet she does not ask now, where is my father, are we to go on this long journey to a distant land without him, for she has come to accept, with the uncanny malleability of a child, that they are somehow peripheral to his existence, even though he might suddenly drown her in a sea of kisses, and on rare nights home, tell a wonderful bedtime tale, spend hours with her drawing rabbits and fish with crooked feet, an image he had retained from a French schoolbook, *est-ce que le poisson a quatre pattes?* he would ask her teasingly, and she would push him away, don't be horrid, you're horrid, horrid, horrid, he will never hear those delightful modulations of her voice again, I have sacrificed you, she murmurs, you have been sacrificed. For perhaps, in the years to come, her father would have been a more valuable mentor, while she fell further into the shadows, for already he took great pains in her intellectual development, gathering fodder for her imagination from the most unlikely sources, here, he would say, on a summer morning, before rushing off to work, when the whole day stretched out before her and the child like a fresh field, here, he would say, handing her a clipping of some Flemish monster he had found in some inscrutable advertisement, when I come back tonight, I want you to tell me a story about this creature, where it lives, what it eats, and then he would return deep into the night, his mouth rimmed with dark pleasure, and bending over to kiss her sleeping head, his eyes would fall perhaps on the crumpled clipping that she had held fast in her little hands, waiting for him to return, and whether his eyes then misted with rare tears, she did not know, for she would be heating dinner, and he would come down, washed, serene, in the embrace of some deep dream. And then there was the time when he had insisted on subliminally subjecting her to classical music, would leave her instructions to bathe the nursery in sweet strong strains of mild baroque, that she might imbibe a predilection for classical music, that later when she took piano lessons, her fingers would move spontaneously to the movements embedded already in the vast caverns of her subconscious. On summer afternoons, the child would come to her and demand that her boredom be broken, and she would be at a loss, where her father would never have failed, on summer afternoons that stretched like a field of sunflowers into the soft evening, in Burgundy, we saw a river of sunflowers, and I wished to sail downstream over a bed of sunflowers, cool against my fingers, years ago, we sailed down the Ganges, you at the prow, training the long lens of your camera upon my shy form at the boatman's feet, for even then, you thought that it was enough to capture me on film, affix me onto celluloid, a tender tropical memory to lie coiled with the smell of old stone in a broken Islamic tomb, the great tree under which we ate, and somehow she had not been able to bring herself to wash her mouth out in the bushes in his presence, she drew a wet hand over her greasy lips, he proffered a milk-white tissue, but she wiped her hands on her sari and folded the tissue carefully and secreted it within her blouse, to draw out later and inhale the hidden fragrance of baby breath and gentle dead flowers within its smooth folds, as she would sniff from time to time the still unopened face fresheners that her aunt kept for her from her airplane flights, cachets that she piled in the back of her desk drawer, only one of them had she dared open, the paper inside was stiff as bird bone, but still bore the faint but sharp scent of airplane eau de cologne, she had longed then that she might wake one day, ripe with the sweet odor of death, the smell of marigolds after rain, and some young poet would bury his face in her hands and grow dizzy from this epic perfume, in the days of yore, a young ferrywoman allowed a sage to violate her under a cloak of mist, that she might be rid of the strong odor of fish that clung to her since her birth, for she had been conceived in the body of a fish who had accidentally swallowed the seed of a king who, overwhelmed by thoughts of love, had hastily ejaculated during a royal hunt and ordered a bird to transport his seed to his queen, and the bird, attacked on his journey, had dropped his burden into a river, and from this ferrywoman indeed their whole race was born, she who had permitted an ardent sage to spread a veil of thick mist in which to take her by, and surfaced still a virgin, mother of a poet, and beautifully fragrant, Anna had been mesmerized as her brother, eager to demonstrate the depth of graphic detail in their epics, launched into this tale, while her ears flamed to hear him speak with such ease of matters condemned to silence in their youth, over fish curry, he had told them of their ancestress who had emerged ambrosial from illicit love, and suddenly it had become unbearable to her that clouds of nectar seemed to be gathered upon Anna's flushed neck, while her skin trapped a stale damp, like old biscuits, in her armpits, the smell of fungid milk powder, and although she had, for the moment, shaken off this obscure insanity, she had soaked long in her bathwater that night, and yet when she closed her eyes, she felt herself to be drowning in the dank waters of a pond choked with hyacinth, the turbid breast of the Ganges, upon which they had floated from squalid Tribeni, where three great rivers had once met, to the church at Bandel, in the terrible heat of late summer, one by one they dropped into hazy sleep, her brother, Gayatri, Tapan, Manash. Amrita was not with them, she remembers, one by one the rest had succumbed to the torpor of the great river, but she had stayed awake, her eyes smarting in the monstrous heat, she had conversed with the boatman, while upon the prow, he sat, with his back to the sun, and his sharp profile against the burnt chalk sky had inspired within her a delicious fear, someday we will die for each other, she had longed to think, as he helped her up onto the slippery bank, his fingers knotting around her like a noose, he seemed in unusually high spirits as they wandered in the church, atrociously decorated, and afterward while they negotiated with rickshaws to cycle them back to the suburban rail station, Gayatri, with motherly solicitude, pulled her up onto a seat with herself, lest the young foreigner, drunk with heat, should see to it that she shared the uncomfortable ride with him, and riding into the sunset, she was content, on that day, a month before he would take her in his desperate arms behind the water tower, a month before that night of fire and thunder, she had been content that none of this would ever go anywhere, even if, with the heat thick between them on the boat, she had longed to think, we will have to die for each other, someday.

And why, today, on the day that my life is to be wrung dry of all memory, why do such images steer strong in my consciousness, the child sits with her chin in her chest, submitting slowly to her strange fate, once you were wrenched from my womb with less violence, she thinks, against my will, my muscles tightened within me, and you were forced to flood your lungs with painful air, and hours from now you will descend into the sulfurous brine that is the air of my polluted home, perhaps like her mother, she will have to sit late into the dark with her, soothing her tired chest muscles with hot mustard oil, for as a child she had suffered from a weak chest, kind neighbors brought strange leaves to be crushed and eaten with honey, that would leave her bilious for days, a grim great-uncle once took her to see a famous homeopath in Shyambazar, for hours they sat in his cobwebbed waiting room, grimy glass cabinets concealed ancient jars bearing moth-eaten labels with enchanting names in faded ink, Arnica, Nux vomica, Belladonna tincture, and vats of miniature sugar balls, congealed now, forgotten, these balls, fresh ones to be sure, steeped in delicious liqueur, were measured out to her every evening, then, for years, to hold under her tongue, precious beads, if he can't cure you, no one can, the gruff great-uncle had forecast ominously, the half-blind homeopath who rubbed his chitinous fingers up her neck and asked her to break the dusty silence of his dim chamber with a cough, and then in a strangely feminine hand wrote a flowing prescription on a scrap of gray paper, to be filled by his apothecary, next door, she had been surprised when the young man, the apothecary, placed in her great-uncle's hand a tiny corked phial of sugar beads in thin liquid, and from then on, for years, the old man would make this arduous journey alone to the northern reaches of the city, to fetch her monthly supply of exotic sugar balls, pure white in the clear sea of herbal essence, but somehow, they had not worked, and one evening, her mother told the old man, not unkindly, not to bother anymore with the medicine, she can still remember the pain in his eyes, for with the years, and with retirement, and with his pension still pending approval, much of that notorious gruffness had worn off, quietly he placed the last phial upon the coffee table, and she had felt then that she would gladly have taken those humble pills for the rest of her life, if he would once slap his knotted hand upon the table and declare, if he cannot cure her, no one will, but he sat in silence, his hands closed over his ivory-handled walking stick, a relic from his extravagant past, it was rumored that before the War, he sent his laundry to Paris, she would wonder then of how he could bear to set his lovely mahogany cane upon the pavements, among the dung and the calf-spittle, the crushed rodent skulls, graveyards of thick insects, and the drainwater that overflowed the narrow street in Dhakuria where he rented a house with his nephew, every monsoon the bottoms of his pressed trousers would be lined in dark sludge, that evening, as he sat with his eyes upon the floor, the helpless phial of medicine upon the table, she longed to press her hands upon his creased forehead, smooth the few hairs that fell limply upon his bald pate, but she did not dare, nor could she bring herself to lie, much as she wanted to, when, suddenly lifting his gaze from the floor, he demanded of her, have they taken you to some other doctor then, she nodded helplessly, the glittering formica of the chambers of a local homeopath, who prescribed a chalky powder corseted in paper sachets, this he claimed was much more effective than the sugar balls, but even it failed to tame her rebellious chest, a series of strange remedies followed, someone even suggested an amulet, stuffed with magic herbs, and that was when her brother had rebelled, even if it does cure her, he told them, how am I expected to reconcile my thoughts and beliefs with the idea that my sister has been cured by magic, witchcraft essentially, even if it did work, it was not worth his intellectual discomfort, nor hers, for by then she had discovered the romantic angle to respiratory diseases, felt a certain kinship with consumptive poets, wished to wither slowly, the delirium of breathing at last after a long night of struggle, she felt, was what fueled the ecstasy of poets, the tranquillity that follows a storm *Like rose leaves with the drip of summer rains . . . fruit ripening in stillness . . . a sleeping infant's breath,—The gradual sand that through an hourglass runs,—A woodland rivulet,—a Poet's death.*

The child has fallen asleep, curled upon the seat, an unintended tranquillity pervades the drama of their journey, she cannot resist the soothing image of the little cheek rising and falling to the rhythm of the pistons, she might as well be curled up in the backseat of their Volvo, her father and his lover in the front seats, she cannot shake the desiccated peace that would have enveloped her then, returning from a weekend outing, the child asleep, fed, ready to be lifted in his strong arms, up the stairs, undressed, still sleeping, and then tucked, happily, happily, into her bed, she cannot rid herself of this thin contentment, within her the tension of her departure fades, lost in the wind-less mazes of unbidden association, a pentimento of painless blue, and in place of the excitement she cannot force herself to feel, a surgical disdain unfolds, dipping deep into the over-whelming discomfort that the earlier part of the day has passed not in sweet slow deliberation as she had planned it, not with the cruel dignity of charred passion, but in a flurry of fast-forwarded motion, a silent comedy feature, outracing her emotions, to be rudely suspended now in the languorous London traffic, as a rapid brook might meet a stagnant pond, now the day refused to pass, although she glanced anxiously at her watch, it reminded her all the more that there was time, time enough to wend like a scurvied elephant through the clotted streets of the great city, time enough to snap with careful fingers the glass threads of her determination, time enough to tap the driver on his shoulder and say, I did not mean, no, I did not really mean that we should come this far, perhaps if we could turn around now, and yet her life here is already part of a distant past, already embalmed in bitter herbs, consigned already to a formless space between sleep and laughter, a tedious pièce de théâtre seen many years ago, from which only a faded resentment for the characters remains, I cannot recall the details of your face, she mutters in sudden delight, the child stirs and whimpers, and then she sees again, in strong soft colors, his head against the girl's, while with her on his lap, they peruse a large art book, Leonardo da Vinci, perhaps, and the child's fingers race madly, in sweet delight, over the pages, it is the gloss of the paper that fascinates her rather than the languid mystery of the broad virginal brows, let it be so, he had told her, when she laughingly brought this to his attention, somewhere within her she will retain these images, and they will come back to her again and again, for he had undertaken to fashion her dreams, so perhaps she will wake within the clammy vapors of a wet tropical winter, her dreams cluttered with women she cannot remember having loved, places that she has never been, perhaps she will be drowned, as she grows older, in memories of a past that is not hers, as she herself had foundered in the vast darkness, aching with desire for men who had passed from this earth long ago, and of men who had never been, perhaps it was that which had ultimately rent them asunder, that it was only ghosts that she could love with wild abandon, and he was flesh and blood, yes, flesh, but that, too, she had taught herself to crave, desert sand, blue in sunset, had inundated her dreams, in the month they had been separated, many years ago, when she had squandered her meager savings upon an airline ticket to Calcutta, it was not a taxi she took then, but a bus, and he had been with her, a delicious sorrow deepening as they approached the motorway exit to Heathrow, they nursed the shreds of this dense melancholy, for it had been long since they had felt united in such emotion, in these last months he had been terribly restless, at night she would wake to find him standing at the window, staring upon the acid streetlights, she had feared that it had all become unbearable, and every morning, in Calcutta, she would wake, terrified that a letter might arrive, or a phone call, quietly telling her that she ought perhaps not return so soon, I need time, she had heard him mutter often, in his agitation, and she had trembled with fear, he began to listen to a strange restless music, from his youth, he explained, they made a trip to Bristol for the express purpose of bringing back old records, with strange sounding names like Al Di Meola, Chick Corea, and suddenly familiar among them: Spiro Gyra, *Spirogyra*, whose curled chloroplasts twisted around her nightmares on the eve of every Biology exam, Spiro Gyra? She wiped the dust off the cover, Trevor would have to transfer them onto tape, for they had no record player, but it was not mere nostalgia that gathered in thick clouds upon his closed lids as he sat on the floor, playing the same tape over and over again, his back up against the wall, temples throbbing, and more and more often, he would tell her, I love you, in a voice sugarpapered, thick with blood, he would tell her, I love you, and the words hung poised upon the edges of a lake of disbelief, he would take her trembling hands and kiss them with excruciating sadness, not the glad passion with which he would smother them earlier that year, heavy with the dream of some other woman, in these last few months he had acquired the appearance of one who was being gnawed alive from within, is it the thesis, she had heard Trevor ask, no, he would say, I don't give a fuck about my thesis, you know that, and once she had heard him whisper, I feel sometimes that I am not living, and she had bled deep, still cloaking her sorrow with sunlit smile, you are my angel, he told her with frightening earnestness and sea-flung despair, she wondered if some woman had refused to love him, was it the love of a woman that was killing him, if only he would tell her, she would soothe his eyes, pierced with night, there was a certain beauty in that, the series of halfhearted obsessions had certainly come to a dramatic halt, perhaps some bright eyes had unexpectedly penetrated to the core of his soul, and then turned away, if only he would unburden himself to her, she would be content to sit by his side and ease his suffering, for the pride of martyrdom ran deep in her race, only she could not bear to live without him, on the morning of her departure, seven years ago, she woke, at dawn, from familiar nightmare, his sad hands traveled down her hair like falling leaves, and as they ate breakfast, slowly, for they had woken far too early, a sweet sorrow took kernel, they savored its tender wind, until, suddenly, before she passed through into duty-free darkness, they had stood horrified while it contracted and died dry upon lips brushing tearstained cheek, and his eyes before they vanished behind the glass were sanded with despair, despair that her absence would bring boundless relief, not the pure grief he had once nursed against the tropical darkness at the very thought of being apart from her luminous eyes. And, later, in the raw milk of winter mornings, amid the dawn cries of the shivering hawkers and the stamping and snorting of tethered cows, the agony of his flesh would engulf her, the warm fields of grass that had drowned her once as he drew her face upon the expanse of his chest, spreading her thick hair upon his rock-veined arms, her hair sank into the sand of his belly, wandered hesitant into fern furrows of his groin, knotted wood flesh, her hair dipped between the blood iron of his thighs, he lifted the dark fronds to his face, they fell into the hollows of his eyes, between the parted lips, rain rippled, in the smoky tropical winter, she woke, suffocated with longing, and turning her face to the wall, she resolved to desire ghosts, once more, to wake with kisses of darkness, flower-washed dew, upon her lips, to drown again in the warm winds of desert cathedrals, lifting gouged eyes to unseen skies of deep burnt blue.

A patch of insignificant green offers respite from the hem of cars, the taxi glibly intercepts a red vehicle, button-nosed, to sidle against the park, upon the rusty rails this edict droops: please do not feed the pigeons, they are a health hazard and a nuisance, once she had reached into a sparrow nest that clung to the harsh cobwebbed slope of a ventilator shaft in the wall of their house, she had reached in, while her brother held her high, and emerged with two small speckled eggs, gray as mottled dung smoke, she kept them in cotton wool, locked away in her drawer, with her diaries, squid-shaped wasps' nests, she found them, years later, on her only visit home, the frail pollution-colored eggs, smelling of dry pondscum, and dreams of ghosts had not come easy, that winter, lost as they were in the thick mists of earthly delights, betrayed, the white mornings curled away in ephemeral wisps, and the day approached when she would return across the seas to her new home, the faded skies recoiled, and she wondered why, in the four weeks she had been there, no one had asked her to sing, that night, a week before she was to leave, once again, she sat, in the dark evening, with her harmonium, moldy now, whinging decayed syllables of sound, she abandoned the instrument and sang long into the night, her brother, a stiff shadow upon the bed, and in the living room, her parents, silent, the hapless fluorescence that flowed through the half-closed door to the bedroom ceased with the usual power cut, as she had hoped, a rich winter dark engulfed them, buoying her song, and as before she sang of love, when love had gone, although before, she had sung of love, when it had never been, and darkness, her old lover, paused among the shadows to listen, but her painful phrases could not hold him, he melted quickly into the borders of the kerosene lamp, the watery fluorescent tubes shuddered into existence, and her voice was drowned by the copious strains of film music from the revived television sets, she pushed away her harmonium, sell it, she told her mother, sell it, it's useless now, and that night she slept in a cocoon of thin clay, a week later when he took her in his tortured arms, his lips tasted dull, and in the year that followed, the clay thickened in great veiny knots, but the ghosts remained far away, in the year that followed, a year of great change, that washed in mute waves across her, moving from the cold flat into the sunny house upon the hill, and the curious contrast of her new job translating the medical complaints of Bangladeshi patients that drove her to the pits of squalor that they called their homes, and he, smiling sardonically as she packed his index cards, the rough sheafs of paper, into cardboard boxes, that she kept in the room where she laid out the new ironing board, no longer would she have to push away his books to lay blankets upon the table to iron her long saris, and sometimes he would kneel down among the boxes, and her heart would flutter, thin cracks in dry wood, but he would

rise, his eyes dead, drained, his work was eating into him, he told
her, give me time, he said, the old litany, but there was no pain
within him now, only harsh cinders, his work exhausted him, and
weekends of do-it-yourself, sometimes the long sweep of his
arm, flecked with creamy white, as he drew a thick brush across
a wall, would stir forgotten longing, a dull pulse of desire, they
would make quiet love upon the covered furniture, and on weekend evenings there were parties, where he would stay close by
her, drinking steadily, his eyes strayed no longer upon the shoulders of other women, and so the days passed, in clouds of light
luminous dust, until one evening, at a strange gathering in Lewisham, of which she can remember now only the large pitchers
of bright green glass, in which they served warm cider, there, he
had come face to face with the daughter of the poet, and a vast
wind had risen from the depths of his eyes, as if it had been
gathering for long in the bottomless shafts, the quiet that she had
mistaken for the steady somber melody of their mature lives was
revealed to her, in that instant, as the caged calm before a storm,
and still the ghosts that she craved remained aloof, until she
began to forget them, one by one, all except darkness, her first
love, still haunting her now and then in the mockery of shadow,
teasing her from within the folds of thick curtains, under sheets,
as he had done when she was a child, she had feared him as well
as loved him then, her first playmate, darkness, and now as cloud
gloom gathers in slow circles upon London skies, she feels a
trickle of his presence beside her, behind her, while the taxi
dives in upon the motorway, and her life is caught once again in
a massive stream of impatient motion, river of crushed sunflowers, and darkness slips away again, amid shaky spasms of sunshine, will he return, and still there is time, a viscous stream,
straining forward, taunting, she may still turn back, although she
feels wiped clean of her life here, cauterized, she struggles to
remain poised, for too much distance will color memory sad

sepia and she will convulse upon the smell of lazy apples and warm hay, the dark hairs upon his arm matted with paint, liver pâté in the garden, the print of Danaë in their bedroom, a shower of gold between her thighs, the unfettered island wind, ripping through old trees, and the trees, the trees, oak, maple, chestnut, oases of elm, the knotted wood veins of his arms, speckled with paint dust, trees destroyed by wind, the new sunshine faltering upon toothless earth, withered violets, papery iris, dried among silver, tarnished eyes, dark as dead wax, and the last blue gasp of candleflame in the wind of a cathedral, the naked sea, spitting black seaweed, and mute mermaids that rose forth from the dark foam on needles of glass, sea pebbles, smoother than eggshell, heavy in her hands, mermaid breasts, spilling salt sea froth, eggshells flaking paint, watercress in the window, wild heath pond fringed by luminous rushes, ducks, foul geese among the violent yellow of new daffodils, the woman upon Oxford Street crushing ice cream cones to feed the pigeons, they are disgorged upon the dull tarmac, Terminal Two, Departures.

The glass doors shut of their own accord behind her, sealing her in, the child hovers alongside, pushing silently at the luggage trolley, she joins a haphazard queue, but impatient hands, uniformed, walkie-talkied, whisk her into another line, less amorphous, she stands, suddenly exhausted, the airport din sending long echoes within her hollow insides, if he were to appear now, and gently take her hand, lead her back, she would not have the strength to protest, and now they are commanding her to unlock her cases, they rummage through the jumbled clothes, the child retrieves a pale rabbit, rudely squashed under red Wellingtons that she would outgrow soon, she turns accusingly to her mother, the red Wellingtons are inverted and shaken vigorously, a dead moth falls out onto the scratched metal, satisfied, the man closes the bags and binds them with yellow tape, now, she is free to queue for her seat aboard the aircraft, and surprisingly, this takes little time, a large medley of trolleys and individuals seem suddenly to leave in unison, an Armenian dancing troupe, someone explains, and her path is clear, she is face to face with the tight-lipped stewardess, who runs a lacquered nail over her passport, their passport, official umbilical, never to be severed, nonsmoking? she nods slowly, and watching the suitcases move sadly away upon the conveyor belt, branded and sealed, trussed with yellow tape that protests their innocence, she is filled with an indescribable loneliness, a bitter sense of failure, she is returning home, the child is blinking, shaking sleep from her large eyes, she takes her hand, behind her impatient travelers shift upon their feet, two women are discussing loudly the presents they are taking for their families in Calcutta, the pujas are next week, they remind each other, of course, every autumn she had watched the city burst into joy to welcome the Goddess Durga to her father's home, and that year, ten years ago, the sad bold shadows of his eyes had widened the sensual exhilaration upon the autumn winds, she had stood under the wide canopy and let the violent drumbeats overwhelm the pulsing of her blood, she had looked for him in the crowds that swirled about her, and when he appeared, with her brother, with their friends, she would turn away hastily to face the wild eyes of the Goddess, the two that blazed upon the demon she had tamed with her many spears, and one that lay upon her forehead, gazing contentedly upon the world, and four days later, cast upon the polluted waters of the holy river, the third eye would stare up at the placid skies, the bride would return, they had stood upon Rashbehari Avenue, his harsh breath upon her hair, they had stood and watched the processions of young men carrying the Goddess to the river, they moved along in bizarre dance, twisting their hips to the adulterated rhythm of cheap film music, this year she will return with the Gods, a daughter come home, this year she will stand captive to the wild, laughing eyes of the demon, many years ago, in the early light of the day, she had stood freshly bathed, upon the rough earth, with the other women she had held to her breast a handful of flowers, while the priest murmured incantations, she had felt his eyes upon her and she had asked the forgiveness of the Gods, and while other women tossed their flowers at the feet of the images she had pressed the soft wet petals to her burning skin, she had let them pour over her own fevered body, this year she will throw them bitterly upon the feet of the Gods, the dull eyes of the feeble men that had once loved her will be upon her, why had none of them dared to inspire such desire within her, why had they let her go, lowered her gently upon the waters so that she would never spill her milk upon the soil that had nourished her, the soil from which they crafted the gentle limbs of the Gods to melt in the acid swirls of the polluted rivers, sinking slowly into the waters on their long journey back to their real home, and yet she fancied that the third eye hovered long upon the turbid surface, pleading with the autumn skies.

The stewardess hands her two boarding passes, she moves languidly towards the escalator, her bones feel heavy, lead-lined, as if the tendrils of this land were pulling at her feet, finally pleading with her not to leave, an indifferent parent suddenly entreating a prodigal child, as the escalator lifts her upwards, she turns to contemplate, through the stretches of glass, the gray sky that has always ignored her desire to spread herself thin upon its arms, ever since that first day, when she lifted her eyes to the distant dense blue, bent double and shivering under his overcoat, sore from a sleepless flight, the sky that did not linger even until evening, and later, she sat, watching dawn break grudgingly through the thick curtains in Trevor's living room, and when they were flung open later, she had

· 174 ·

gasped at the indifference of the sky, the mesh of cloud, stretched thin, like a beggar's rag upon the pitiless blue, how will I love such a sky, you will find towels in the cabinet under the sink, Trevor enunciated carefully, and from the bathroom window, tilted open, she scrutinized the distant blue again, the smell of burning bacon curled in from under the door, along the wall, by the time they set out for Paddington, the sky had taken on the color of dead grass, darkening in yeasty gusts, and from the train window, she watched the hasty sunlight slip away, leaving watery dark, and the occasional island of light scum, petty conurbation, and finally, Bristol, her heart rose in a great leap to her throat, here, somewhere, under sullen British soil, lay a man who had transformed the destiny of their race, Raja Ram Mohan Roy, whose more extreme disciples had flung beef bone and chicken bone and unholy onion peel into the courtyards of Brahmans, had died here, under incurious skies, more than a hundred years ago, and as she washed dishes, later that evening, he promised her a pilgrimage to his grave, he stood beside her, smiling, stroking her hair, while his mother stiffly dished the remains of her tasteless casserole into the garbage bin, and her eyes had lifted to the steam upon the pale tiles trapping faint flower forms, bloodless phantoms of flower, drained of desire, she had fancied that somewhere nearby, upon the feckless dark, roamed the spirit of the man whose secular dreams fashioned the poet's God, by the hissing gas fire, she fell asleep and dreamt that he had come to her, in the pancake hat of her history book, and he was telling her she had forgotten the sugar, what sugar, and suddenly warm dry hands were upon her, dry lips upon her forehead, go to bed, love, her helpless sleeping image had uncorked a sea of emotion within his mother, there was another she had not had the courage to bid farewell, the silent woman in her silent home, always suspicious, it had seemed to her from the very first, of her son, she had been shattered by his adultery,

she remembers, overhearing in the room beyond, surfacing suddenly from the drowning murmurs of the child sucking at her
breast, across the thin walls, the dry voice of his mother, I will
not have her in my house, Anna on the telephone from London
confirming that she would join them, please, mother, calm
down, she can hear you, the child began to cry, and a few
minutes later, he came in to kiss her, I have to go to London, I'll
be back tomorrow, he kisses her over and over again, and the
puckered face of the baby, spilling milk bubble, the front door
shuts with an angry bang, he is gone, and his mother wringing
her hands upon the kitchen table.

And then suddenly, the last flecks of stone fall, she is pushed
headlong into a tunnel of blackness, clutching the child, through
passport control, the deed is done, there is no turning back now,
in this way, she had turned away from the faces of her mother,
her father, her brother, Sharmila, smiling fiercely, many years
ago, the same dense uneasiness had edged her excitement, this
is death, she had thought, the snub-nosed airplane that had
waited to lift her into the clouds, they disappeared from her
view, merged into a wall of waving arms, only the tomato-red
shorts of the neighbors' son signaled their presence, years ago,
she had carried herself up the steep metal steps into the saccha-
rine cold of the airplane interior, this is death, she had thought,
he had stroked her trembling cheeks, and she had seen in the
hollows of his thoughtful eyes, death, a sweet alternative to life,
for she had loved him then, and although, perhaps, even as the
aluminum wings sliced through the moist tropical air, their passion had begun to die, she had never dreamed that one day,
years later, she would have the presence of mind to walk out of
his life, he who had pounded into her salt flesh in such sweet
agony, the space between them was too thick with secrets for
her to wrench herself away, even if he should find bliss in some
other woman's arms, for even then, in the first few days of their

love, even then, it had seemed clear to her that he might not be satisfied with the pure agony of their lust, but she had thought then that even if it should come to that, they would be bound by a deeper experience, or at least she would live forever for the mere touch of his fingers, like thunder upon her skin, she would sit and sing into the darkness until he returned, his desire renewed by the inadequate stiffness of another woman's limbs, she had thought then that she might let him feed upon her wakeful anguish, the cold flesh of dawn would wrap them in dense delicious sorrow.

Unshackled misery, cold metal upon her tongue, why has she left him? He who held her young limbs with sleep-soaked fingers, many years ago, the morning after their wedding, he who had buried his smoldering eyes within the pale sleepless depths of her skin and told her he would never know such happiness, it should have been enough to shift the last embers of such passion between her numb fingers, and wait to die at his side, to be buried deep in a foreign soil by his grave, so that the dust of their bones might mingle and fertilize the same bed of grass, instead her ashes would scatter upon the fetid waters of the holy river, and he would wither without her, and yet she had dreamt as a young girl, before she had known that she might tread upon these chalky shores, she had dreamt then of wandering as a spirit with her beloved upon English moors, her hot tears had spilled upon the yellowed pages, she had loved Heathcliff before she loved any man, and she had let a sweet weakness grow within her, she had convinced herself amid the long shadows of a tropical summer evening that she would never be able to leave any man that had loved her, that she had once loved, and today she submitted to the probing cold of the airport metal detectors, the bewildered face of the child beside her, and wondered where that peaceful conviction had floundered, and drawing the blankets upon her within the airplane, she sensed within the rough distant touch of cheap wool the beginnings of a sensual languor, an odd craving for his hot flesh that would sustain her for the rest of her life without him, after years of indifference at his side, for the first time a rush of warmth sweeps between her thighs, she remembers the flecks of burned skin upon his shoulders, many years ago, in the tropical sunlight, the morning of their departure, in the room that she had shared with her grandmother, the beds had been pushed together, discolorations in the concrete floor revealed their original arrangement, she remembers his sunburned neck, turning slowly towards her, you have not slept at all, it was her last night, they had sat and talked, her mother, her eyes black with grief, her father, waking from sad fits of exhausted sleep to join in their wistful conversation, she and her brother horribly awake, and towards dawn only they remained wide-eyed, while others snored, a penetrating embarrassed silence had erected itself between them, to-morrow, he said, flatly, you will stand above the Thames, you will see the Big Ben, she had smiled falteringly, and then Bristol, he said, and turned to face her, and almost sneering, he said, but no back to Bengal for you, the faded half-curtains flapped against the window bars, the first sickly rays of the sun filtered through like sugar water, somewhere a cat gives a blood-curdling shriek, in the last film they saw together a kitten was used as a paperweight, does he remember, dada, but he stood up and brushed past her, she heard the aluminium edges of the bathroom door grate upon the rough floor, and she had walked slowly back to the room where her husband slept, she had sat by the household shrine, where the gods were tucked safe into their beds, ants crawled upon the unwashed bell-metal plates upon which they had been offered sweets, the day before, and on that final morning, while he still slept, she had watched through the mosquito netting while her grandmother prayed, the sweet stench of tropical flowers, and then for the last time her grandmother had reached through under the netting to daub her parting with vermilion, casting a disgusted look at the pale man by her side, the curious eyes of the maid, scrubbing the speckled concrete floors, peeped over the carved bedboard, and she had pushed his freckled fingers away, as he reached for her in his sleep, those same hands are sliding down the white gloss of the closet doors, empty closets that she has left behind, in futile disbelief, his nails bend against the eggshell firmness of the paint, the clean edge of the door cuts into the salt-stained shadow of his cheek, inside the blackness is hard, amorphous, if she had died while he had still loved her, he would have come back to a moth maze of gauze and silk, steeped with old naphthalene, this she had imagined, in her first British winter, weak with bronchitis, while she lay against the pillows and he cradled her chin in one hand and fed her warm soup, she had thought then, if she should die now, he will clench in his crazed palms the forest of clothes that she would wear no more, bruise his lips upon the rough gold thread, drown his misery in the wail of tearing silk, if she had died while he still loved her, and if she had died, as she thought she surely would, in the strange still hours between the pangs of childbirth, she had feared then that the anguish might have fed their passion, the poetry of her motionless garments in the unused closet, bittersweet tears would smudge upon the forlorn shadows, he would have let them hang forever behind the cold doors, and from time to time, heavy with the love of another woman, he would bury his face among the embalmed folds, he is staring now into the darkness that might have been her shrine, his eyes are like pale moonlight garroted by cloud, she turns away from their futile shadows to the cold hiss of sugary air that comes down upon her face from the vents above, a fly crawls up the curved wall, they will be here, long after we are gone, Trevor told her, as they watched dung beetles struggling with balls of excrement, perfectly formed, like a fried sweetmeat between its pincers, she dug her toes into the frugal sand, upon the mat, they rested, under olive

trees, Trevor spit out a pip, he read from his book, *and Rosel*
speaks of a German who was in the habit of spreading spiders,
like butter, upon his bread, she had watched his shoulders heave
with laughter, at her feet, those shoulders trembling now,
against the lonely shadows of abandoned toys, in the child's
room, the music stops suddenly downstairs, the first layer of the
parcel is unwrapped, a thousand small whispers rise up with the
warm air to meet his muddy eyes, the music starts again, he
begins to laugh, she shudders and turns away from the pale glow
of the sunset they are rushing to meet, the night that they will
escape, would you like wine with dinner, the stewardess asks,
she shakes her head, *Back to Bengal,* the child stirs, plump
fingers clutch at the baleful stuffed rabbit, earlier this morning
those fingers were stained with watercress, her little plot will lie
untended under the tall windows, *Under sleep, where all waters*
meet, Bowsprit cracked with ice and paint cracked with heat, I
made this, I have forgotten, she sees him on his knees before her
bed, the eiderdown rising and falling under his heavy breath,
hard sorrow glistens upon the eyes that pleaded with her once,
against the damp light of the kerosene lamp, to come forth into
the insect-laden haze so that he might drink of the misty hollows
sculpted into her flesh by the rain-ravaged dark,

> a devotion into which has faded the sad perfume of fallen spring
> flowers
> a devotion that has imprisoned the rhythm of a poet's heart
> this you did not know
> I kept your name hidden under colored shadows, you did not
> know

Back to Bengal, and the Sanskritized romanticism of Bankim
Chandra Chatterjee, the nineteenth-century novelist whose
books she had fed upon, one long hot summer, when she was
twelve, the complete works that nestled behind the glass doors

of her uncle's bookshelf, gathering cobwebs, concealing mis-spelled love letters to a cousin married off long ago to the man-ager of a tea estate in the hills, it must have been sad, she had thought, to belong to a household where one could hide things in books, or had she hoped that someday, someone would find them and read of the fruitless passion that some unworthy young man had cherished for her, she had replaced them, trembling with young emotion, she is curious suddenly to see if they are still there, the ink, rotten with age, smelling like menstrual fluid, she had let a baby spider crawl upon her fingers, on the night that he had held her for the first time under the canopy of fireworks, she had set a tray of biscuits upon a kitchen shelf, and her hand had come away with a tiny spider, she had watched it skim across her palm, while he waited upstairs upon the roof terrace, tenderly, she had released it into the gunpowdered darkness outside, shaken the sticky threads from her fingers, soiled with his breath, she had seen herself then, growing old without him, upon the red soil of the poet's home, that was where she resolved to spend the rest of her days, at the poet's school, she would hold her memories close in the dry Birbhum cold, on sparkling mornings, the students would lift their eyes to watch her recede into the sparse palms, and on clear evenings they would stop by her window to absorb the pure sorrow of her song, overwhelmed by the beauty of her loneliness, they would forget to chew upon their consonants, that distinctive accent that her brother's friends mimicked, and on festival mornings, a si-lence would fall, as she reached for the harmonium, under the pavilion where they gathered, the skies would reel under the echo of her song, the students would whisper later, among the dew-laden creepers, they would whisper of a lost love, an Englishman that she had never followed across the seas, she would pass like a stern shadow under the angular murals of the blind painter, blindness, he had said, was a new experience, in the documentary they had watched on videotape in Amrita's husband's study, the week before, she and Anthony alone, while the others argued over her brother's adaptation of a Dario Fo play in the room beyond, she hung on to whiffs of their conversation, as the servants passed with tea and coffee between the rooms, anxious that they should appreciate her brother's work, waking from dreams of love she had watched him, wrapped in a faded shawl, upon her grandmother's bed, a rare sight, for him to be awake before her, he who often snored until noon upon the living-room divan, immune to the myriad morning movements, she had watched him with glad, sleep-stained eyes, bending upon the ragged foolscap. And there among the regal shadows of Amrita's husband's study, as she watched Anthony's eyes flit between the television screen to her anxious face, she trembled that Amrita might tear her brother's efforts to shreds in her measured voice, and then she was mesmerized by the hands of the artist upon the screen, groping with shapes to re-create the tender landscape of his new blindness, blindness is a new experience, and long ago, she had seen the flower girl raise her hands to the Tramp's sad smile, and murmur, yes, I can see now, merciless light, for which the poet had pleaded,

> deliver me now from this darkness
> give me sight
> I will drink gladly of its pain
> for this happiness sits heavy upon me
> let my eyes be washed clean with tears, give me sight.
> The magic of dark shadows beckon, my burden grows heavy with
>   dreams
> let me look upon the light that hides on the edge of night
> give me sight.

One acrid winter evening, while he twisted her fingers into the ravaged hollows of his palm, she had watched Oedipus, King of

Thebes (Manash, chalk-chested), spit upon the sterile agony of the privilege of sight, blindness was the one inalienable right of mankind, and backstage she had wiped the red paint off his lids, Manash had chuckled and chanted out of the nonsense poems of Sukumar Ray that had been the fabric of her childhood fantasies, of the strange custom in the nonsense land of Bombagarh, during full moon, of smearing alta, a red paint that women used to decorate their feet, upon the eyes, as she greased away the tormented blood of the proud king, with his eyes shut, he continued to recite, with exaggerated schoolboy cadence, *And why at nighttime, is the pocket watch steeped in clarified butter, Why does the king use sandpaper for sheets*, the bulge of his cornea darted back and forth under the pressure of her fingers, but my favorite line, Moni, he told her, *Why does the queen's brother hammer nails into bread,* for once, she longed, instead of sharing in their exhausted satisfaction, to be alone to contemplate the terrible sadness of the king, the strange satisfaction of his blindness, all this, and the delicious torment of his hands seeking hers in the rancid darkness between stale velvet seats, she had longed to cry upon his neck for the misery of the king, the cruel hands of fate, whose tendrils she had recently felt, pulling her into a great abyss, and what did one have left then, after all, like the wretched king, bereft of all but his undying sense of pain and beauty, she too would be drawn into some terrible vortex and some self-mutilation would be demanded of her, so that she might retain her humanity, and yet, now, she must wipe the red dye off the actor's cheek, a hollowness engulfs her, never before had she found so wistful the end of a performance, she who had lovingly brushed aside the cobwebs in the wings to edge into the pleasant tumult, she had stood back and inhaled, with indescribable happiness, the moist satisfaction that rose from the perspiring backs of the players, she had leaned against the dusty beams, among meshes of gnarled wires, the vast innards of a thing of beauty, she had knelt to tip the earthenware urn in the corner of the green room and pour water for parched throats, smoothed powdered tresses and wrinkles had dissolved under her handkerchief, and yet her brother insisted that they should take their theater to the streets, dispense with costume, and cease to make fools of the audience, she had shuddered then, although she knew of the strange distance it bred, the impalpable superiority, of having been behind the scenes, the thrill of power, a mockery of fate, and on that evening, as she rubbed away the remaining specks of red from the corners of his eyes, she had recognized a certain honesty in the concept of a performance without secrets, without costumes, the drama of the backstage had faded to sullen anticlimax, she wished to be alone with him, who watched her silently in the speckled mirror, in Bombagarh, broken bottles hang from the throne, the king's aunt uses pumpkins for cricket balls, and his uncle dances with a garland of hookahs about his neck, the images fill her with a sudden melancholy, jagged green glass of dusty bottles swaying against the worn gilt of a mad king's throne, the year before, she had gone with the theater group to the pungent alleyways of the Muslim quarters at the great river's bend, to visit the grave of a forgotten monarch, whose kingdom was snatched from under his effete fingers by the conniving British, while his courtiers played chess, the son of the nonsense writer had rinsed the absurd agony of his defeat upon celluloid, and inspired by the film's rich mood alone, they had found his ignoble tomb, and yet they had lingered only briefly in the musty halls of the dead mosque, driving afterwards through the narrow streets to the home of Amrita's household tailor, whom they had paid to prepare them a real Moghlai meal, an orgy of their senses, Amrita had frowned upon the bottles of beer under the seats, and ordered them not to abuse the purchased hospitality of the humble Muslim couple, Moni had held the thin bread to the light, the crosshatch of its filaments cast shadows upon the white tablecloth, what you are about to put in your mouth, someone had said, I think, is the unnamable of a ram, and she had stuffed her mouth with the gossamer bread to obliterate the nausea, her strong food taboos had always been a constant source of amusement, and so Trevor had read with a twinkle in his eyes, his voice caked with the stillness of hot lavender, he had read, *Réaumur tells of a young lady who was so fond of spiders that she never saw one without catching it and eating it, Lalande, the French astronomer, had similar tastes.*

Hours later, the night shadows hang deep in the corner of the airport, while they wait for a connecting flight, sour bread, sour butter, cold eggs for supper, the child still sleeps, as if lulled by death, a young man sits next to her, reading an obese paperback, the child's toy slips from her sleepy grasp, he picks it up and hands it to her with a smile, the dim lights glint upon his glassy chin, he returns to his book, but there is a mild self-consciousness, the irritating tension of half-acquaintance, she pretends to sleep so that he may read in peace, often, on their frequent long drives, she had let her head drop against the vibrating window, closed her eyes and let her tired mind weave through the torpid landscape of feigned sleep, so that they might converse unencumbered by her silence, he and Anna, caught upon the motorway on a Sunday evening, he would reach over to stroke her cheek, then move another few inches on the road, and Anna would play with her hair, the loosened braid flung over the seat, as she pressed her forehead against the moist glass, the toy rabbit slips from her grasp again, before the young man can pick it up it slides across and knocks against a bald gentleman, taking photographs of his family, standing wooden against the harsh light of the duty-free shops, he kicks it away in irritation, the young man gets up to retrieve it, he holds it by an ear, dusting it gently as he walks back, she apologizes and they laugh, he asks her if she is going to Calcutta, he has not been there in many years, he was born there, he assures her, he is going back to do his medical elective at the hospital where his father was trained, it will be an experience, he was a child of two when his parents left, she knows their story, she has heard it many times before, of how they had landed upon English soil with a mere five pounds to their name, the first difficult years, on weekends they had shared curried shad with other couples and reminisced of hilsa fish, cradling their children, they had rubbed their eyes in the damp heat of the coin-operated gas fires, and absorbed heavy texts, and now they basked in their hard-earned success, in detached suburban homes, their children amassing A-levels, she remembers a damp day, in the week that he left her with his mother in Bristol, watching TV with a mug of cocoa in her homesick palms, she waited for him to call from London, but when the telephone rang, it was not him, but an unmistakable East Bengal accent drifted through the spangled wire, you will not remember me, her father's distant cousin, they had urged her to spend a day with them, and the following evening he had driven in from Cardiff to take her with him, with guilt and relief she had waved to her mother-in-law, he asked her many questions during the drive, and in the oppressive heat of their home she had met his kind wife, the smell of fried spice hung dense in the overheated hallway, the wife, her aunt, took her coat, in the living room a large soapstone Taj Mahal stood under a glass dome, after dinner she played Scrabble with the children, you're good, the older girl told her incredulously, and later as she looked out of the guest-room window onto the lights of industrial Wales, she felt strangely trapped. The following morning, she sat with her aunt upon their bed as she sifted through a bundle of old clothes, take these, you will need them, believe me, it doesn't make sense to wear saris always, and yet within her advice there was a certain hesitation, a delicate awe even, she had, after all, married an Englishman, and she had been consumed by a sudden impatience to be back within the still cold walls of his mother's home, to count the hours until the weekend, when he would return to take her back to the great city that she had only briefly seen, whose streets, childishly indifferent, she had longed to love, the musty caverns of its underground veins, echoing the brittle melodies of a thousand fearless flutes, dog spittle and lush weed upon grimy pavements, last week a man had knocked upon the door and asked if he might weed the ragged border against the front wall for a little money, she had stood silent while he searched her face with hopeful eyes, the eyes of a tired reptile, darting back and forth across her face, she remembered the silent agony of a frog that her cousin had tried to pith unsuccessfully, many years ago, on vacation with her aunt in rural Bengal, the cousin had found the unfortunate amphibian upon a muddy road, and determined to dissect it, he had brought it back to the bungalow, there upon the long veranda, while the asbestos eaves vomited rain, in the absence of chloroform, he had drawn out a sharp tool from his dissection kit, which he had faithfully transported from the city, and asking her to read the instructions from his laboratory text, he had held the poor beast down, while the rain spray speckled the thin, glossy pages, she had read, and he had driven the sharp instrument into the frog's head, the maid, who had come to clear away the grass mats, had fled in disgust, and alas, the poor creature was not knocked painlessly into a stupor, but instead squirmed dreadfully in his hands, she had shrieked, and he had driven deeper, desperately, and then, unable to bear its suffering any longer, he had flung it far into the dense rain, to drown in the clotted mud of the thick puddles in the fields beyond, and a thin ghost of guilt had hung over them both, that evening, as they dug dully into their rice and lentils with rain-wrinkled fingers, the stainless-steel plates gnashed upon the damp floor, her brother teased them about their cruelty, she whimpered and swore never to have anything more to do with cutting up animals again, her cousin sat silent, and the following morning he came back across the sodden fields from the science teacher's house, with a small dark bottle of chloroform, and in the early afternoon, two small village lads appeared with a sackful of toads, he gave them a rupee each, he released many of the toads, she watched them hop away, impressing upon her, once again, how utterly arbitrary were life and death, and then, while the household slept, and she wrote her journal upon the stiff bed, he pinned the anesthetized beasts to a waxed tray and snipped away their skin and muscle, the smell of watery toad blood mingled with the fetid odors of baking mud, the sun shone harsh, she declined his offer to come and watch its beating heart, it can feel nothing, Moni, believe me, but she refused to look upon the pulsating muscle, months later, she would draw the organ in his laboratory notebook in her careful hand, and write in the enchanting labels, sinus venosus, the merciless rhythm that would haunt her for a long time, the young man taps gently upon her knee, time to go, time to kiss the soil of Europe a last farewell, and far far away, he is staring, in cold, mad anger, into the crumpled ruins of the birthday party, the last child leaves, unaware of the existential satire they have unwittingly become part of, a birthday party without the birthday girl, the birthday cake lies uncut, among the mess of sandwiches, jelly oranges, and cold custard the sugar rabbit lies, indifferent, candles poke into its fur, he breaks off the tip of one ear and laughs a hollow laugh, the child settles sullenly into her seat, I want to go home, she says, but then she finds a source of unending delight in the mechanism of the seat belt, the resounding click, the sudden release, she giggles, and the young man leans forward to smile at her, his arm touches hers and a sudden sharp warmth condenses within her, she draws her blankets up to her chin, this is absurd, he is but a boy, besides, all these years, she has remained hopelessly immune to all fond caress, the fervent fingers of the young American upon her hands were like knotted spiderwebs, Anthony's guilty hands upon her breasts awakened no desire, those hands, crashing down, now into cracked icing, dark cake flesh, salt tears mingle with fat raisins, and later he will sit upon the stairs, his fingers stiff with sugar, and stare upon the deep red welts on his lover's waist, chafed by the cruel gold threads of the garment lent to her, as once the harsh embroidery had eaten into her own young skin, while he tussled madly with the strong folds of cloth that hid her thighs, darkness had watched disdainfully from the foot of the bed, the lights dim within the airplane, the warmth of the young man's arm presses through her blanket into the ridge where her arm falls against her side, she fancies it is darkness, her old lover, enfolding her once again in a graceful lust, the gentle sweep of incorporeal desire, fine moth wings across the nape of her neck, with her face to the smoky winter night, the bus rumbled down Dhakuria Bridge, and darkness had reached for her out of the crowd of bodies bearing upon her, the odors of fresh winter sweat upon musty wool, darkness had lain quiet, trembling fingers upon her burning shoulder, cold lips had searched through her tresses, fogged with sick sweet incense from the joss sticks that burned against an image of Mother Kali above her seat, dim lights twinkled in the shanties that girded the railway tracks, then on Anwar Shah Road, where, once, not so long ago, foxes had roamed, and the ponds nearby were thick with skulls of young revolutionaries, there the bus had screeched to a halt, and disgorged her into the arms of darkness, and with him she had walked down the dim streets, past the cruel ponds, choked with water hyacinths, hiding the young bones of those that had fallen, not so long ago, and the city had wiped them from its memory, except in hushed mezzanine rooms where brothers, beaten brainless, waited for a tardy death, and in the bitter poetry of defeated spirits, and although their name brought a strange thrill to her blood, stirred a deep compassion, their philosophy remained shrouded in a haze, to her, she who had sensed only a vague current of fear, in those troublesome times, while her mother lifted the tired curtain and waited, as the sun grew weak, for her brother to return, but in those days, he had been a quiet, almost affectless lad, politics and art were very far from his mind, then, he who would later write of their struggle, their merciless extermination at the hands of the State, he had been indifferent, then, while they were dragged out and filled with bullets beside rotting ponds, he had read his schoolbooks, and now flimsy apartment buildings stood upon the slime that covered their bones, darkness had breathed upon her neck as she climbed the unlit stairs, her body hung ripe under his touch, bursting against the seams of her blouse, yet it was as if he were preparing her for someone else, someone who would come with the spring, to whom she might have whispered:

in the dying light of that March day
I saw in your eyes, my doom

but he came with the rain, on a night of dark thunder, he came to her door, his knees swept with rain slime, his toes rimmed with black mud, his eyes washed clear, he had looked upon her in the hazy lamplight, and she moved away into the damp shadows and promised to darkness, as she had once vowed to the poet in the shock of learning that he was mortal:

if the doors to my heart should someday close upon you
break them down and enter my soul, do not turn away
if on these violin strings your beloved name does not play

still, I beseech you, do not turn away
if someday, at your call, I remain encased within dead dream
wake me with the agony of thunder, do not turn away
and if someday, upon your throne, I seat someone else with care
remember, you are my only king, do not turn away.

And yet, somehow, on that winter night, the year before, as she climbed the darkened stairs to her uncle's new flat, she had felt in his impalpable caress the sweet anguish of farewell, I leave you with a song of spring, with time you will forget me, and yet on spring nights, the sorrow of this song will shroud your eyes with tears, she had turned horrified, to face him, but the piercing sweep of torchlight from upstairs had hidden him from her, Moni, is that you, her aunt called, can you see, take care not to fall, and he had emerged from the shadows to follow her up the last few steps, I have left you with a song of spring, I do not wish to stay past my time, and yet as she felt the last tendrils of darkness crawl away from her, a strange hope engulfed, a wild expectation, that a storm would rise to befriend her, she looked back into the sparse shadows, A new spring will come, and from the lips of a new wanderer, a new song, she walked up into the light, Moni, you should have yelled from downstairs, her aunt said, I would have sent someone down with a light, the house-warming ceremony is over, the religious runes upon the door will be washed away tomorrow, the blessed earthenware jug, squat, upon the floor, a dense perfume of new whitewash hangs in the air, she presses her burning palms against the clean, chalky walls, she is a woman who has waved a last goodbye to her lover, and today, in the tinny shadows of the airplane cabin, he is back with her, strange sharp currents well in her arm with his touch, but he is a boy, with his hair slicked back like his trendy friends, yet his face is narrow like a poet, eyes deep, brimming with an amused desire, she will share his hidden laughter, she lets the blanket slip off her shoulder and shakes her head so that her hair falls from the bun onto his arm, he trembles under the weight of her tresses, as darkness had trembled beside her in the tropical winter stillness, darkness, her true love, her only friend.

The poet's songs were collected into those of devotion, and those of love and nature, earthly delights, the distinction confused her, many a time she had searched futilely among the love songs for one that lay buried in the volume of devotional lyrics and yet inspired within her a deep physical longing, beyond the thin line that divides death from life, you stand, my friend, she had dignified her parched desire on evenings, shut in her room to practice her music, with songs that the poet had offered to his God, give me not merely your poetry, soothe me with your hands, how do I quench this deathly thirst, the fatigue of this long road, oh, the darkness is full of you, grace me with your touch, my friend, my love, my heart longs to give, not merely to receive, it breaks under the weight of all that it has gathered, give me your hand, I will hold it, fill it, keep it close, this long and lonely journey I will fill with beauty, lay your hands upon my soul, beyond the wooden shutters the car horns blare, the children come home from the park, their knees blotted with dust, to this she will return, the pale streetlight slides through the shutter slats disturbing her tryst with darkness, an evening coolness begins to spread through the concrete floor, the raucous notes of conch shells diffract the silent shadows upon the walls, all over the city hasty evening prayers are being muttered before the television soaps begin, to this she is returning, the beloved tropical dusk will murmur once again in her ear like the frantic thoughts of a mute poet, for this she has left him staring into the moth-veined darkness of the spaces she no longer occupies, the sour memory of a child's laughter, will he come to claim her, or will he let the days pass, until one morning, seized with an unbearable guilt, he will sit down to write to his daughter, and the ink will dry upon his pen as his thoughts twist and turn within him, he has become, in the space of a few hours, an irrevocable part of an unreal past, he has been engulfed by time, he sits in the shadows of the monstrous toys upon the stairs and he remembers a night, many years ago, he stood back against the wall to allow them to pass with his sister upon a stretcher, once again, he has been betrayed by those he loved most, and most neglected, she feels no guilt, as her hair tumbles upon the trembling shoulders of the young stranger at her side, she feels no compassion for the sorrowful eyes from which she is rushing away at a speed beyond that of thought, only a gentle scorn for the depth of his disbelief, a blast of cold air sweeps into the hall as Anna opens the door to leave, let me know when they come back, she says over her shoulder, he does not answer, the door shuts, he will sit long upon those stairs, in the watery darkness, a numb sleep will conquer his bewildered mind, and from this he will wake, out of cardboard dreams, he will wake to the insistent peals of the telephone, his mother, anxious, grim, brimming with silent admonition, and then he will wander, a defeated ghost, among the ruins of the surreal birthday party, like the skeleton of a play he might have written, his hands deep in the pockets of his overcoat, which he has not taken off since he walked, earlier, to watch for them from the top of the hill, while the party merry-go-rounded within his home, he will sit by the table, his hands deep in his pockets, until, listlessly, he reaches to lift a small drooping sandwich to his lips, break off a corner of the shattered cake, he will taste wax among the cold sponge and he will remember the warm tallow between her fingers, the night of fireworks, their first night of love, he will roll the bitter crumbs against his palate, while she watches the dim necklace of lights unfold below, her city, unreal city, a deserted carnival, they land in the forlorn mist of an early autumn dawn, and his eyes, already rust, merge with the hollows within the face of darkness, his smile melts in thick rain, as would the lips of darkness, when she turned to face him in storm, memories of pitted stone, his teeth, furious upon her tongue, come washed now in fragrant moss, he is there already among the familiar phantoms that rise to meet her as she drags the sleepy, silent child down the rickety steps, into the air, thick with ghosts, carnival players, past their prime, dragging swollen feet, destroyed poets, fingering death, brush by her like old felt, and among them, her old lovers raise tired, happy eyes to welcome her, and he is there, incorporeal, the deep hollows of his eyes obscured in astringent tropical mist, and yet he leads her tenderly through the glass doors, he looks on, smiling, as the passport is fingered, and sweat whorls mingle with ink, upon the flaky blue page, by the sluggish conveyor belt, his inchoate presence stirs a vast green pain, as darkness battles with his shadow, and smiling he shrugs him off, as he had done, on the night of their wedding, burying his fire deep within her, he had ignored darkness, standing betrayed at the foot of the bed, his presence condenses beside her as she watches the luggage moving in endless circles, unclaimed, and yet, as she steps outside, he is lost quickly in the harsh new light of the tropical sun, already marching upon the pavements, he founders in the sea of humanity that rushes to smother her, taxi, madam? her cases are snatched from her hands, the young man waves from within a crowd of relatives, perplexed that there is nobody there to meet her, a boy loads the bags into a taxi, beggar children tug at her and ask for foreign money, the taxi moves with strange lethargy into the damp morning, gathers speed upon the tree-lined stretches of pockmarked road, the child stares, wide-eyed, she asks no questions, a lime broth of sunlight is boiling inside the taxi, the sweet stench of burnt rubber wafts in through the open window, a wetness grows where her arm rests against the vinyl seat, the morning mists burn in small sighs under the autumn sun whose rays prick her neck like gentle reeds, the wind smells of watered honey, soothing the acrid condensation of thick exhaust that blows in from the bus that staggers ahead, the sugary effluvium will stiffen her hair, as it did years before, and she had held her head under the fierce spray of the shower, until her hair formed a slate wall between herself and the world, behind which she might dream of his eyes, the distant flame of burning cities, abandoned to the night, will he remember her as she will, crushing sour sheets in her palms, she will remember how she had come to enjoy the depth of his lust, as she had learned to love violet, the color violet, with its aspirations to darkness, like the shallow black of faded night, she had come to love violet as the color of lust, and the many dawns, when she lay awake, staring at his broad back, darkness had deserted her then, she had crushed a chalky violet upon her palate, and numbed by its sudden rich sadness she had forgotten to hold the taste within her, so that she choked only upon a cold thin infusion, the dregs of violet, and today her eyes fall upon the circle of the horizon, where the violet of the sky battles with the lime of sunlight, and this fills her heart with joy, on the Eastern Bypass, vultures circle over the tanning fields, the driver apologizes that one of the windows does not roll up, she smothers the child's nose with a corner of her sari, the girl sneezes a small sneeze, the vultures hover above the buttered winds, once, she walked upon the parched breast of a great river towards a pack of vultures conferring upon the sandy riverbed, bare-headed, they had scrutinized her, as she approached, and then, wearily, they had left, one by one, lifting their wizened flesh into the skies, the taxi turns away from the silent road, the Bypass, circumventing the arteries of the city, they had come, to the South, her home, they had chosen the bright silence of the Bypass, the fetid air of the tanning fields, rather than the convulsed alleys of the crumbling North, where the heart of the city had once lain, when the poet was born, in eighteen hundred and sixty-one, he came into the vast shadows of his father's great house, north of the city, a pilgrimage they had made every year, in the searing May heat, to celebrate his birth, large crowds gathered in the courtyards where he had chased his brothers, upon the long verandas where he had sighed when out of the pouring rain, a despised tutor emerged shaking his umbrella, and somewhere within these vast shuttered rooms, a deep burning had weaved within his young veins, his eyes had rested desperately upon the quiet beauty of an older brother's wife, and thus their race had been permanently infused with the deep tragedy of incest, gathered on dark nights, they whispered of his doomed passion, and dreamed of forbidden love, her schoolmates, the taxi drives past the bus stand, where they had waited after school, to see off those that took a bus home, before they began to slowly walk back in the sticky afternoon light, cross the tram lines, as the taxi does now, into the narrow winding alleyways where once a friend had stood horrified while a dead sister's lover declared his passion, in that very snack bar, they had pooled together their meager finances to share eggrolls, the road is blocked by a large bamboo frame, the skeleton of a canopy for the Gods, men are decorating it with folded cloth, tomorrow the images will appear, a thin perfume of festivity streams into the taxi, they reverse into a driveway, above them, a woman parts the washing to dispose of a ball of hair, it falls stealthily from the balcony into the gutter, she looks upon a strip of dying grass, where once, many years ago, she had talked for an hour with a friend's beloved in their newly acquired French, *qu'est-ce que tu manges pour le petit déjeuner*, lesson twelve, and he had replied, twisting his young beard, *je mange des chaussures, comme Charlie Chaplin*, and her friend had never forgiven her, standing aside, excluded from their satisfied laughter, that year he left for university in the United States, and years later, in the winter when she came back, alone, for her only visit, she had gone to their wedding, they lived in Chicago, or at least they had been there, there had been a letter with a Chicago address, but she had not replied, its conspiratory tone had annoyed her, brimming with pride that the privilege of living in the West was theirs alone among their group of school-friends, the radiant ring of faces, some newly married, others patiently waiting their turn, she had seen these faces, smudged with ink, pale with nervous perspiration before an exam, she had seen them last, at this wedding, in the winter when she came, alone, for her only visit, wrestling to reconcile her existence within this city with her life in London, the blue chill of the morning, cold library ink, and in his dark eyes, the anguished recognition of the passing of desire, watching the holy flames flicker upon her friend's bridal veil, a deep nostalgia had taken root in her, like her, she too had one day placed her painted hand in the trembling palm of one who longed deeply to drink of her existence, and in the years that had passed since, she had watched that desire fade into a beloved dream, would he re-member her, as she would remember him, like the deep dust of old incense within the white walls of a Himalayan monastery, like a silence that was there before the forest in which it is trapped, for even before she had looked upon his face, his mem-ories had pleaded with her, in the rusty tropical darkness,

Even so, remember me
If I should move far away, even so
If the old love should be lost in the mazes of a new passion
Even so, remember me
And if although I am near
My presence, like shadow, is shrouded with doubt
Your eyes might cloud with tears
And if one lovely night this game should end

Even so, remember me
If, on an autumn morn, the final blow should fall, even so
And if, remembering me, tears do not come
Tears do not glisten in the corners of your eyes
Even so, remember me.

Intoxicated by nostalgia, she leans out to contemplate the skies, from behind tall shutters, the reluctant strains of a thin child voice float down, faltering in the crevices of one of the poet's most difficult songs, shrill, flat, it fades pathetically away into the paused sunshine, the taxi grinds to a sudden halt, upon Rash-behari Avenue the water main has burst again, they say it is the curse of the Ganges, whose old course ran through that very spot, the wheels rock upon a bird carcass, crushing crow flesh into hot tar, upon the streets, early crowds are gathering, she looks upon the faces of a generation who knew the poet only by the dregs of his dreams.